SWIM COACH

A GREENBRIDGE ACADEMY ROMANCE

ABBY KNOX

Edited by Aquila Editing
Cover Designer: Mayhem Cover Creations

This book is dedicated to the bulge. We see you, we acknowledge you, we love you.

SWIM COACH

BOOK ONE IN A COLLECTION OF STORIES FROM GREENBRIDGE ACADEMY

By Abby Knox

Admired, overachieving high school senior **Addie** has turned 18 and plans to wring out every last drop of her elite private school education. When a school legend returns to coach her swim team, however, her composure waivers under his stern gaze.

Coach Ford doesn't lavish anyone at this school with the praise they are accustomed to, and Addie isn't sure what to do other than work harder, and swim faster. If she could only manage to keep her head down and keep her wet and wild fantasies under control...

The majority of this book is told through the eyes of the heroine, with occasional, brief glimpses from the hero's perspective. The wonderful, steamy, funny, sweet, smutty payoff is worth every tear-stained page of teenage longing!

Fair warning: this is a borderline-taboo story in which a student falls for her coach. All main characters are consenting adults. If power dynamic is your jam, then this is for you!

Not ready to go back to school? This stern, bronzed god with the whistle says **YES, YOU ARE!**

ADDIE

THIS MORNING, like every Saturday morning for the last twenty-plus years, my mom and dad are drinking coffee and sitting together on the sofa listening to public radio.

Their dorky routine makes me smile. Remembering how much I adore them helps me say what I need to say.

"Mom? Dad?" I breathe in, noticing my stomach churning and my palms sweating.

I clear my throat.

"What is it, sweetie?" my mom asks as she curls her legs underneath her, a pose indicating she knows I need to talk about something heavy and she's ready to listen. "Zeke, can you...?" She motions for my dad to turn down the volume on the radio.

He nods. "Sure, honey."

"Um...well, I'm 18 now...and I have been thinking of making some changes this year at school," I say.

"It's OK, Addie," Dad says with a smile. "We're not going to bite your head off."

Don't be too sure about that, Pops, I think to myself.

"Well, I've decided not to go out for the swim team this year."

Both my parents freeze, their coffee cups stuck in mid-air, halfway to their lips. They look at each other. They look back at me. They seem unsure how to react, and in their discomfort, they laugh. It's not a derisive laugh, it's more like an "I don't know what to do with this information" kind of laugh.

I clear my throat again. Their faces register that I'm serious. Mom asks, "Why in the world would you quit the swim team? You went to state last season. You're filling out college applications."

Dad interjects. "This year is going to be huge. You definitely do not want to quit. The athletic director is bringing in Weston Ford to coach."

The sensation in my body at the sound of that name is nothing more than dread. That's what I tell myself. It's not schoolgirl butterflies. It's simply not.

No other athlete brought more acclaim to my school than Weston Ford. A phenom his entire career at Greenbridge Academy, he led the varsity swim team to four state championships, then went on to do the same on the national level in college, and even competed in the world championships. I'd heard whispers about him trying out for the Olympic swim team. Whenever the subject of Greenbridge swimming comes up, it's only a matter of seconds before Weston's name is mentioned.

I can't imagine what kind of money the school board offered him to get him to give up competing to coach here.

Weston Ford was the reason my best friend Hunter and I tried out for Greenbridge swimming in middle school.

Hunter and I both had our eyes on that boy since our preteen years. He was five years ahead of us and a regular lifeguard at the city pool. He was so cute in those red swim trunks and white sunglasses, with his bullhorn and whistle and that hint of a smirk whenever Hunter and I laid out our towels on the hot concrete pool deck just inches from his tall lifeguard chair. And that tan. My god, the way that boy imprinted on my preteen brain — not to mention libido — was almost criminal.

Hunter would drool over his abs and shoulders. I was hypnotized by his masculine legs, which he let grow hairy in the off season.

Kids at the pool were afraid of him. I wasn't scared—I was fascinated.

But there is no way in absolute frozen-over hell that I am going to let that man coach me now. Our team doesn't need to fall back on the past to win a championship. It seems to be backward thinking to me.

I take another deep breath. "That's just the trouble," I say. "It's like a bad movie reboot. It's not fair that they fired Coach Judy. It brought down the morale of the whole team. Everyone's upset."

Dad cocks his head at me and speaks as warmly as he can. "I know that Greenbridge is tough on swim coaches. But we are the best private K-through-12 school in the state, with a top swim program. If a coach can't produce state titles consistently, that's the end. Judy was good, but she wasn't great. Our swim program isn't good, it's great, and we need a great coach."

My parents, especially my dad, love to talk about Greenbridge swimming like they are an active part of it. He sips his coffee and waits for me to speak. Mom looks worried.

"I realize all of that, but...I don't know anymore. The athletic director took the wind out of our sails. It just seems so small and petty in the whole scheme of things. A high school state title doesn't really mean much in the long run, does it? We're not curing cancer or ending poverty."

My mom finally chimes in. "You might be surprised by this, but I agree with you to a point. But while we're talking about the greater scope of things, remember that swimming is going to play a huge role in what college you get into and what scholarships you may receive. And with a good education, you might have a better chance at solving the world's real problems, yes?"

Always the philosopher, my mom wins this round—in theory.

In practice, not so much.

"I've made my decision. I'm quitting the team in protest. And so are Hunter, Ridley, Hadley—everybody. And you don't have to worry about scholarships. I'm an adult and I'll figure it out."

2

ADDIE

AND SOMEHOW, I'm here.

The faint scent of chlorine in my nostrils fills me with dread and despair. At one time that smell, the feel of this humid room, the echoes of the laughter of my fellow teammates filled me with excitement and anticipation.

Today, it all adds up to bone deep anxiety.

I do not want to be here.

And yet I am. How did this happen?

"Thanks for compromising your principles, my friend," Hunter says as we stretch each other's arms in the pool. "My parents laid down the law. There's no way I can not swim my senior year and have any hope of getting their help to pay for a good theater school."

I shrug. The way I see it, she doesn't need their help. She's a shoo-in and has plenty of options to get financial aid. I said as much to her when she texted me that she'd changed her mind about the protest walk-out.

Turns out, pretty much everyone's parents had the same reaction as Hunter's parents.

Based on the chatter I hear around the pool deck, it sounds like I was the only one who didn't have to back down.

My mom and dad had simply said to me, "Well, honey, if you feel that strongly about it, we can't stop you."

Thirty minutes after my well-rehearsed and thorough argument as to why I was quitting the team, I donned my green swimsuit from last year, matching school logo swim cap, and goggles.

I'm starting to wonder if they knew all along it would turn out this way. I wonder if all the swim parents are in a group text.

I could have said no to Hunter, but I'm here because no way will I stand by and let her navigate the season alone. She's a much better swimmer than I am, but if I followed through with quitting the team, it would mean abandoning Hunter to the mercies of our team captain, Ridley Rushmore, the biggest queen bee that ever buzzed around Greenbridge Academy and maybe its best female swimmer ever.

"I wonder where he is," Hunter says.

"Where *who* is?" I ask, feigning stupidity.

She snorts, knowing I'm pretending. "You're adorable," she says. "I mean, Weston Ford hasn't been around Greenbridge in four years. I wonder what he looks like now."

I laugh, pretending I haven't been looking up videos online of his world championship swim meets. "Probably the same, but with a much bigger cranium to carry around his huge ego."

Hunter laughs. "I love you."

"And I, you, my dear."

Hunter and I first met at pre-K when Matthew Jensen

told me I could only play with the pink Legos. When I cried, Hunter walked right up and body checked him with her pint-size frame, scooped up all the Legos into the front of her dress, which she held out like a bowl, and marched them over to me so we could play with them ourselves. She and I have been inseparable ever since.

We hear Weston Ford before we see him. It begins with a whistle—a long, sharp whistle. We all stop what we are doing and whip our heads around to find the source of the noise.

In the microsecond before we all spot Weston standing on the concrete steps leading to the men's locker room, my subconscious's hard-wiring sparks to life.

That whistle. *Oh god.*

I'm transported back to the summer before eighth grade, hanging out at the public pool with Hunter, trying to impress the aloof lifeguard with our new pink bikinis. We'd bought the skimpy swimwear on the sly with our babysitting money and hid them from our parents.

The commanding, shrill whistle flips some kind of switch in me. And then I lay eyes on Weston.

Hunter gasps quietly.

As for me, I don't make a sound.

He's four years older now, and his hairy legs are somehow even more toned. The years have bulked him up into a full-fledged adult man and carved his face into an impossibly more stern look. As a teenager, he'd always let his sun-kissed hair flop into his eyes, surfer style. Now, he sports a short, low-maintenance cut that complements the strong lines of his brow and the set of his square jaw. Summers spent under the sun are catching up with him, giving his eyes the faintest hint of crow's feet.

"Everybody out of the pool!" The bullhorn crackles. "Hornets, line up!"

His voice contrasts the shrill, yet inexplicably arousing, whistle. Bullhorn distortion aside, his voice is deep, gravelly.

My pulse quickens as he descends the stairs and I take in the whole picture. The whistle jostling against his bare chest as he moves. The fitted, Euro-style swim trunks in signature Greenbridge green. A clipboard in one hand, a bullhorn in the other, and, for a touch of nerdiness, a No. 2 pencil tucked behind his ear.

The bullhorn crackles to life again as we scramble out of the water. "Line up behind the platforms! Alphabetically by last name."

So loud. So abrupt.

And somehow, something dormant inside me is waking up and saying "Yes, please, and thank you."

My stupid nipples are hard and begging for attention like a couple of problem children.

I'm last in line. I pass closely by him while he watches us move into order. The proximity affords me the pleasure of noticing the beads of water all over his chest, shoulders, and trickling down those amazing legs. Clearly he's just come from the shower, and he smells like a woodsy kind of soap.

Do not picture him in the shower. Do not picture him standing under the hot spray...eyes closed...lathering up... soapy tendrils cascading off his erect man nipples. Do not wonder if he showered with or without those grown-ass-man swim trunks on. Of course he put on the trunks first. Who wants to struggle putting on fitted trunks over a wet body?

I blurt out a snort of laughter. Everyone turns to look at me. I turn pink and wish for the pool deck to crack open and swallow me up.

"Say 'here' when I call your name." He sets down the bullhorn and scribbles something on the papers attached to his clipboard.

After he calls each name, Coach Ford glances up quickly with a disinterested expression to confirm each team member is present, checking them off his list one by one as we respond.

"Dana Bayside... (check)... Daphne Degrassi... (check)... Maria Lawndale... (check)... Hadley McKinley... (check)... Claire Ridgemont... (check)... Ridley Rushmore... (check)... Hunter Rydell... (check)... Adelaide Shermer..."

"It's Addie," I say, clearing my throat.

His eyes stay trained on his clipboard.

"Roster I received from the athletic director says your name is Adelaide."

For one long moment, his eyes look up to connect with mine. He doesn't look away, even while he takes a moment to tuck his pencil back behind his ear.

For the rest of the day I will analyze the meaning of that look. Is he annoyed? Exasperated? Cautious? Curious? I can't tell. Of course, I've no idea that moment will set the tone for my entire senior year.

Regrettably, my voice comes out breathy and I speak in the form of a question. "That is my name, but everyone calls me Addie?"

What's wrong with me? I never talk like this. Why is my voice doing this?

"In my pool, everyone goes by their last names anyway. Any more information you need to share with me, Shermer, or can I move on?"

"Uhm..."

But before I can reply yes or no, he turns from me and

sounds his whistle. "Rushmore! Fifty freestyle. Show me what you got!"

Ridley's tall, lithe body barely makes a noise as she hits the water. Watching her swim is like looking at art; her body seems to skim through the water with no resistance. There's a reason why her 100-meter freestyle is the second fastest in the state.

By the time she hops out of the pool like a ninja, I feel like maybe I should not have spent the whole summer working the counter at Yum Burgers and sun worshiping at Hunter's house.

Ridley's super-rich dad probably hired a private coach, because her form is even better than I remember.

Of course, she has every advantage. Hunter's parents may be affluent, but they're only doctor and lawyer rich. Ridley's dad is next level— he's hotel magnate rich. We've all benefited though. Mr. Rushmore bought us our own special activity bus —one for the men's teams and one for the women's. He's probably responsible for recruiting Weston Ford, too.

Our new coach makes no comment about Ridley, only looking at his watch and scribbling on his clipboard.

One by one, he goes down the roster and makes each girl demonstrate her strongest event.

When he barks out my name, I barely hear it at first, I'm so lost in his hands and the way his big, strong knuckles forcefully grip the pencil. And the way his brow furrows as he writes, the way his jaw ripples while he watches each swimmer's form.

"Shermer! Breaststroke! Fifty!"

The breaststroke. Of course. My worst event. Why?

I look to plead with him to pick a different stroke, but he's not even looking at me. His eyes are on his clipboard, and he's just waiting for me to hit the water so he can push a button on his watch.

I dive in and get it over with. It takes about a hundred years to swim to the other end of the pool and back. If Coach Ford were not waiting on me, I would have been bored out of my skull.

I hop out of the pool and keep my eye on him for any sign of how I performed. I see nothing—nothing except one eyebrow move maybe a millimeter. Barely there, but I saw it.

And because I can't leave well enough alone, I stand there dripping while filling the silence with my babbling.

"I'm the weak link in the breaststroke. I suck so bad at it."

Slowly, Coach Ford slides his pencil back behind his ear and stalks toward me. I swallow and try to tamp down the panic rising in my chest. Is he going to shout at me?

When he reaches me, he clasps the clipboard with both arms over his midsection and stares me down.

I might melt on the spot. If I were not dripping wet from the pool, I might think I was turning to molten liquid under his fierce brown stare. Brown...with flecks of gold. Oh lord, help me. He's so pretty.

He raises one hand and points a finger so close to my face, I could easily lean forward and suck it into my mouth if I wanted to.

I don't want to. Do I? What I want is to dive back into the pool and hide in the drain at the bottom of the deep end until everyone leaves.

He does not shout at me. Rather, he speaks calmly and with authority. "No one. On my team. Is a weak link. You got that, Shermer?"

I get it so hard I feel it thrumming in the darkest, wettest place of my swimsuit.

I swallow and nod.

He makes it worse by saying, "Excuse me? I didn't hear that."

"Yes," I squeak quietly.

"Yes what?"

Yes what? What does he want me to say?

I suppose... "Yes, sir?"

"Are you asking me or telling me you understand?"

I clear my throat and lift my chin as I spit out. "I understand, sir!"

He nods, then moves on to the next task.

I'M SO SHAKEN by him that my stupid brain dreams about him that night. In it, Coach Ford is spanking me with a clipboard, punctuating every slap with a whistle. I startle myself awake to find I'm rubbing my groin against the mattress to create delicious friction. An involuntary tightening and releasing is accompanied by extreme relief and pleasure crashing through my body.

Did I just have an orgasm?

More to the point—did I just have a wet dream about my swim coach? Oh god. This season is going to be even worse than I imagined.

WESTON

THIS GIRL—THIS woman—has a passion for swimming.

The way she speaks, moves, swims—everything—it's like she's wearing her heart outside of her body for everyone to see. She's got the heart of a champion and she doesn't even know it.

Adelaide Shermer.

I see from the files that Judy left in my office that she's 18.

Not that it matters. I'm her coach, and I'm only here for one reason: to lead Greenbridge Academy to a state championship title.

And Adelaide is going to be the key to bringing it home.

ADDIE

BY THE FIRST day of my senior year, we've been practicing for a month.

And the wet dreams about my coach have not stopped. Even when he shouts, blows that whistle, barks at us with the bullhorn, my body reacts in mysterious ways.

All my life, my parents, friends, teachers, and administrators have fawned all over me. Given me encouragement. Built up my self-esteem.

And I appreciate that.

So do I need therapy? Why in the world does my heart race, my palms sweat, and my pussy walls throb with arousal when Coach Ford does the opposite? And why do I get more aroused the angrier he gets during practice?

At least school will give me something else to focus on.

Hunter snatches my schedule out of my hands while hanging at my locker first thing in the morning.

"What does the Queen of Advanced College Credit have on tap this semester? Basket weaving?"

I laugh and roll my eyes. "No! Just some electives that I never had the chance to take before.

Hunter shakes her head and looks up at me. "Advanced Psychology? Trigonometry II? Girl, that's just more college cred," she sputters.

I snatch it back. "That's just a bonus. It's fun and interesting!"

She sighs. "Well, at least one of us has brains."

I playfully slap her shoulder. "Hey, don't talk about my best friend that way. You finished all the drama and music courses this fancy school has to offer and this year they had to make something up for you. Shall we talk about advanced costume design and dramaturgy?"

She blushes. Hunter is extremely talented and she knows it.

"OK, see you at lunch. I'm just bitter that we have no classes together."

We hug and part ways. We really have been inseparable for so long, it's weird not being able to help each other study. Truthfully, she could have graduated early and gone off to New York to take acting classes before starting college if she wanted. I encouraged it, in fact, but then her parents stepped in with their advice that one more year of swim would make her more well-rounded on college applications.

Later, at lunch, I finally spill to Hunter that I think I had my first wet dream.

"Oh my god," Hunter whispers over our vegan pitas she picked up from a nearby restaurant when she cut out of her study hall early. It's so nice to be able to leave campus to get food. The cafeteria food at Greenbridge Academy is super healthy and pretty good, but it's nice to have some autonomy, finally. And it's nice not to have to eat lunch with the elementary and middle school kids. This school is big on different age groups interacting with each other. "Who was it about? What was it like?"

I bite my bottom lip. "It was a little scary, almost like the big descent on a rickety roller coaster. Maybe I didn't do it right."

She giggles. "What did it feel like at the bottom?"

I sigh and look around in case anyone is listening. "Like a full-body sneeze. But then it woke me up and I felt sad that he...uh, that nobody else there."

Her cheeks pink. "Oh, you did it right. Lucky girl."

I shake my head as the heat rises and reddens my ears. "I don't know if I would call it lucky. It felt...so empty when I woke up."

"Who was it? You have to tell me!"

I hesitate. She's so eager and she is my best friend. But... I just can't. No way am I telling Hunter that the man I pictured in my dream was Coach Ford. I'm not ready yet.

Besides, she looks like she might be hiding something from me too.

"I'm not totally sure who it was. He was big. Tall. And he had nice hands. Kinda mean? But I liked it."

I expect her to playfully call me a weirdo but she only nods thoughtfully. Knowingly. We eat the rest of our lunch while discussing safer topics than boys and our deepest, darkest secrets, and stick to chatter about the royal family. It feels weird. We've both always been a bit boy crazy, and we love to break down everything over lunch. Something is missing and I don't like it.

After lunch I have an hour of independent study, and since it is the first day, I have to meet with my staff advisor. As I make my way to the guidance office, I should be thinking about my proposal for my independent study, but instead my mind wanders to swim practice for tonight.

I wonder if Coach Ford is going to have us practicing the same strokes or assign us new ones. I wonder if he's going to give us pointers. Or better yet, a demonstration.

Even better still, a hands-on demonstration in the water.

The skin on my chest begins to feel hot. My hands become clammy. Parts of me feel tingly. I have to bite the inside of my cheek to make myself put aside my daydreaming about Coach Ford and try to focus on the moment. I say hi to the guidance receptionist, who waves me in.

When I push open the door of the guidance office, I freeze.

What is that scent?

It's a fresh, green, foresty scent. It's like...oh god...but no...there's no way...

I step into Ms. Frazier's office and there, sitting adjacent to the counselor's desk, is...Coach Ford. His eyes are fully trained on me. So much so, it makes me uncomfortable. And I like it.

"Oh. Hi, Coach," I say, my throat thick. Dammit, there's that breathy voice again.

Ms. Frazier clip-clops in behind me in her killer heels. She's so beautiful and sophisticated, I don't know how she's still single. "Addie! Mr. Ford! Good, you're both here. I believe you two know each other. We had to do a lottery to see who would end up with you."

The way she phrases it rings so inappropriate in my head. I repeat it back to her. "A lottery? To end up with me?"

"Certainly," Ms. Frazier says. "All the available teachers were looking forward to see what kind of independent study you came up with, so we literally drew a name out of a hat."

I meet Coach Ford's intense gaze with an awkward smile. "And you ended up with the short end of the stick," I say self-deprecatingly.

The coach's eyes flash with seriousness, bordering on anger—almost the same energy he had at the pool when he corrected me for calling myself the weak link. "Hardly," he says. "Every teacher at this school raves about what a brilliant student you are." Is it weird that I kind of want to hear him say that through a megaphone?

Ms. Frazier chuckles. "It's not an exaggeration. As a matter of fact, Weston, I've been trying to convince this girl to graduate early for a couple of years now."

This meeting is turning into a festival of compliments and it's making me blush. Guess I won't have to worry about impressing anybody with my independent study project idea.

I chuckle and shrug as I reply, "It's true. Ms. Frazier's been trying to push me out of Greenbridge for some time. But there's something to be said for having the full high school experience with my friends, going to graduation, prom, the whole thing. And sticking with the swim team has turned out to be fun, too."

I think this is the first time I've seen Coach Ford's eyes blink and his face soften for me. Is that a smile? Not exactly —it's almost like he's trying to keep himself from it. "I'm happy to help with athletic scholarship applications."

Ms. Frazier laughs. "Yes, I think you got a few of those in your day, Weston."

He chuckles and shrugs humbly. "One or two."

"So tell us, Ms. Shermer, what do you have planned for your independent study?"

I sit up straight in my chair and take out my folder and give copies of my plan to them both.

"In a nutshell, I'm going to follow the city's recycling program and write up reports on how the system actually works, where the stuff actually ends up, and develop proposals to improve the system, wherever possible. Specifically, I'm going to follow one simple piece of recyclable plastic and see where it goes and how long it sits around, waiting to be recycled."

Ms. Frazier sits back in her chair. "Well. As I anticipated, I won't have to worry that you might be using independent study to slack off."

"No, ma'am. Do you want me to go through the outline of steps...?"

She waves me off. "I trust you, dear. Full steam ahead, and I'm excited to see what you come up with. I have no doubt your end-of-year presentation will dazzle all of us."

Coach Ford echoes, "No doubt."

Coach's baritone voice rattles every cage inside me that keeps my inner bad girl locked up tight. I'm not sure how much longer she's going to tolerate being caged.

5

WESTON

I NEVER THOUGHT I'd spend the bulk of my afternoon at the perfume counter at the mall, trying to locate that scent. It's citrusy and fresh, with just a hint of warm, comforting spice. When I finally find it, I know it immediately.

It's *her*.

The biggest bottle they have goes back with me to my office.

I place the tiniest dab of that perfume on the edge of my whistle, which has become a permanent fixture around my neck.

6

ADDIE

WHEN HUNTER and I meet up in the locker room before swim practice, we tell each other all about our independent study projects. She's going to be co-directing the all-school winter musical along with sewing all the costumes. And then for second semester, she's going to be going on actual auditions in New York and Los Angeles if she can manage it.

I tell her who my staff advisor is. She laughs. "Oh shit. Guess you aren't phoning this thing in. That man is going to ride you hard all year long!"

The double entendre gives me a full color daydream of exactly what I should not be daydreaming about.

I feel like everyone can see my thought bubbles and they all know I'm imagining Coach Ford riding me. Or would I ride him? Either way, never have I felt so pure and untouched, so hopelessly inexperienced compared to people like Ridley Rushmore, who has the air of someone who has had tons of sex. And why wouldn't she, since she's been dating the captain of the boys' swim team for two years now? She walks around the locker room completely naked and full of confidence, and even looks like a bombshell wearing her swim cap and goggles.

Swim gear only makes me look like a giant bug.

I need to watch some porn and soon so I can at least know what I'm doing when the time comes.

As soon as I step into the pool area, the heat between my thighs and the pebbling of my nipples are instantaneous. Coach Ford is already there, waiting for us, waist deep in the shallow end. Hands on his hips, he announces to the group, "A lot of you are almost there, but almost there doesn't get us a state title. I'm going to demonstrate each form that you need to work on, and then you're all going to get in the water to show me what you learned."

And then, he swims.

His arms slice through the water, creating hardly any wake. It's almost silent. Every time his arm comes over the top of his head, I get the briefest glimpse of the muscles under his arms, on his upper ribs. For crying out loud, this man has muscles where no other human has muscle definition.

It's so beautiful to watch I could cry.

He barely comes up to breathe. His flip turns are effortless, and so fast. So controlled. So powerful.

After each form, he pauses to explain what he's about to do and what he sees us do wrong repeatedly. He goes through the breaststroke, backstroke, and butterfly, prefacing each with a laundry list of mistakes.

My breathing is shallow and all my blood seems to be pooling in my sex organs. The walls of my sex quiver with lust, demanding to be filled. I've never felt that emptiness before—of wanting to sheath the full length of a man's organ inside my body—and I'm disturbed by this feeling.

Finally after about twenty minutes of this torture, he launches his body up out of the pool.

"Shermer and Rydell, on the platforms. Breaststroke."

Hunter and I walk toward the boards, and just as I pass by his drenched body, I see it.

The bulge is so...there... My eyes can see nothing else.

My heart hammers, my palms sweat. I have to take my eyes off that bulge, but I can't not look.

The faint chlorine smell combined with his masculine scent is killing me. The rivulets of pool water make beautiful designs along his strong upper thighs. I have never wanted to be a drop of water more than I do now.

I force myself to look away, but I instantly wish I hadn't. Now, Coach Ford and I make eye contact, and I feel like my whole face is as red as a tomato. Topped by my Greenbridge swim cap, my whole head must look like a light-up Christmas ornament.

I forget those embarrassing two seconds once I'm up on that platform and staring at the water, waiting for the whistle.

Hunter and I dive in on command, and I proceed to blunder through my least favorite stroke. Coach Ford barks at us. "Watch your shoulders! Breath control! That's not what I showed you! Coming up too high! Not high enough!"

I hear Hunter muttering and cussing as she comes up for breath. She hates this, and I don't blame her one bit. Me? I'm loving it. The more he shouts orders and corrections at us, the more I push myself. The more he voices his frustration and disappointment, the more I want to keep going, to work harder. Something comes over my body, and

I'm going faster than I ever remember going on the breaststroke.

When we finish, he doesn't tell any of us our times were any better than yesterday's practice. He simply disappears into his office and we all meander into the locker room when he doesn't reappear.

When we hit the showers and I peel off my swimsuit, I have the overwhelming need to use the private shower.

"Suddenly shy, Addie?" Ridley drawls in my direction.

"Period," I fib.

The hot spray starts up and I pull the vinyl curtain on my private stall. "I can't believe it's taking so long for all our periods to sync up!" someone shouts.

Everyone laughs before moving on to talk shit about Coach Ford.

"He yells too much."

"He's so mean."

"He's going to work us into the ground."

"That is so not Judy's style."

"What's wrong with him? Why's he such a grouch?"

Let them all hate him. Let them talk all the shit they want. Whatever it is he's doing, it's going to work. Because the only thing I feel is energized. And tingling head to toe.

I wet my washcloth and dip it down between my legs. Closing my eyes, I explore with the cloth all these feelings he has pulled out of me. The heat, the need, the overwhelming desire to be touched.

Of course I've touched myself before, but it's never that easy to find the spot where I'm most aroused. Right now, however, my clit is unmissable. It's hard and needy and begging for relief. I part my folds and rub urgent circles around the tight bud. It's never felt this urgent.

I should not be doing this here. I should wait until

bedtime, where I can be alone, hidden under the privacy of my blankets. But it's too much. I have to have relief now.

I close my eyes and all I see is Coach Ford—his grumpy face and huge, shining bulge and the water dripping down his beautiful legs. Those images, along with the rubbing, set me off without warning. It's so shocking and such an enormous wave of pleasure that I'm not expecting it.

My foot slips off the bench. I yelp as I try to compensate by shifting my weight backward, but my other foot slips out from under me, and I topple to the floor. My hand grabs at the shower curtain as I go, causing the rod, curtain and rings follow me down.

When my teammates come and find me tangled up under the curtain, I lie there like a dolt. Hunter turns off the shower and asks me what happened. Everyone is looking at me.

I lie through my teeth. "Lightheaded. I guess I blacked out."

Hunter helps me up and sets me down on the bench.

"You're getting your towel wet," I say weakly.

"Shut up. Are you OK? Did you hit your head?"

I shake my head.

"I'll go tell Coach," says Hadley.

"No!" I urge. "I'm fine. Don't bother him. I just need some water."

"But she could sue the school..."

"Oh, Hadley! You would say that," says Hunter, referring to the Hadley's law firm family and its long history of attempts — and failures — to force the firing of one Greenbridge headmistress or another over the years. Yeah...this school is full of stories like that.

WESTON

ADELAIDE SHAVED six seconds off her time today, and her muscles are getting stronger, more flexible. She's a beast of a swimmer.

She must already know that.

ADDIE

AT FRIDAY'S PRACTICE, Coach Ford is dressed in a baggy t-shirt and loose board shorts.

Hunter frowns and mutters to me, "Where'd the tight little trunks go to?"

I shrug. I'll admit to myself his new getup is little unprofessional, but at least I don't have to look at the outline of his dick and then nearly concuss myself in the shower.

That night in bed, I ruminate on why Weston might have switched to baggy clothes instead of getting into the pool with us.

Ever since meeting him on the first day of practice, I have tossed and turned at night thinking about him.

It's not fair.

A coach is supposed to be an old, boring adult who wears dad jeans, drives a minivan, and talks about the days before everyone had cell phones and social media. Coaches are not supposed to be unbelievably hot, recent college graduates.

You know what's also not fair? The fact that I'm eighteen, and he doesn't recognize me as a fully grown woman. All he cares about is whipping the team into shape and making Ridley demonstrate proper form. Like she's a freaking goddess of the pool or something. Well, compared to me, she is.

I'll show him. By the end of this season, I'll have transformed myself from the team's weakest link to the fastest female swimmer in school history. Maybe then he'll speak to me like the adult I am. Maybe then I'll be able to speak to him without my voice going all stupid and breathy when he's around.

The truth is, anybody would have the drive to achieve her goals with Coach Ford in authority over them. He's so commanding, it's almost scary sometimes. When he furrows his brow as he looks over our disappointing times, it just makes me want to work harder. When he barks orders at us, my heart hammers, eager to get into the water and show him what I'm capable of.

And, oh god, when he blows his whistle, down-deep excitement blooms inside me knowing his eyes are going to be on me while I do whatever he asks. My craving to please him, to draw those deep brown eyes and severe expression my way, is all I can think about.

Unable to sleep, yet again, I give up. I roll over and pick up my phone and begin scrolling through my favorite social media timeline.

Coach Ford and I are not friends online, but there's no reason I can't creep on his page. I'm sure all the girls do it. Hunter even dared to send him a friend request. I wonder if he actually responded to that.

One way to find out... Unfortunately his privacy settings are such that I can't see who he's friends with. He doesn't even list a relationship status of any kind. Frustrating.

I scroll down, but can see very little. Figures that a guy like that would also be social media savvy. I click on his cover photo, which looks like a group shot of him and a bunch of friends. They all look about his age, and from the surroundings, it appears they are at a concert together. Three guys and three females. One of the women, a redhead about his age, has her arm around his waist. The image shouldn't be so upsetting to me.

But it's not just upsetting. I'm obsessed with it. I have to find out who she is. Is she a girlfriend? Sister? They don't look alike.

I touch two fingers to my phone screen to enlarge the image to look for any more clues about his relationship to this woman. And that's when my finger slips.

Oops.

I gasp and clumsily drop my phone.

Staring at the ceiling for a moment, I can't believe what just happened.

My stomach churns. My heart races. My jaw drops. My face, hands and feet start to sweat.

What. Have. I. Done.

I'll tell you what I've done. I've just "liked" a photo of my super-hot swim coach at 3 a.m. on a Tuesday. My pulse pounds hard in my ears. In my panic, I have trouble finding the button to "unlike" the photo. I finally find it and undo it. But the damage is done. He's definitely going to see a notification about this.

"Way to go, Addie," I say to myself. "That's one way to get his attention."

9

ADDIE

THE NEXT MORNING as I wait for Hunter to pick me up for school, I experience a whole new kind of cringe when it becomes clear that Coach Ford has blocked me on all social media.

I climb into Hunter's new Infiniti and fail to look as impressed as I should.

She counsels me on the way to school.

"Listen. We are goddesses. We hold our heads high. And besides that, there's no way he told anybody about you creeping on his page. What good would it do a teacher to mention to anyone that a female student liked one of his shirtless profile pictures at 3 a.m.? They would be asking, what is Weston Ford doing to get the attention of young girls? Nah. He's too smart for that."

"You're right," I exhale. "And by the way, tell your parents thanks for the upgrade. The other car was beat to shit."

"Oh. Right. Actually, they're pretty pissed about this car because, well, I sort of got my way even after they put their foot down." She bites her lip and seems to be concentrating harder on the road than what is normal for her. I'm thankful for that, but something is up.

"Sounds like quite a story. Care to spill it?"

She takes a deep breath and exhales a dismissive laugh. "Oh, you know, how it is. Daddies can't say no to their little girls sometimes."

"True," I say, still not believing her but changing the subject anyway. "How are things going with the winter musical?"

She nods. "The costumes are coming along. It's a lot of work. But the truth is, I miss acting. And actually that's something I need to talk to you about. I'm thinking of going away for a few days over Christmas. So I won't be around for our annual shopping trip. I ... uh ... I have a meeting with a talent agency."

Shocked by this news, I silently scream while clapping my hands. Finally, I shout, "I'm so excited for you! I bet your parents are over the moon! No wonder you got a new ride!"

"I haven't exactly told them." She shrugs. "They're not excited about my plans to incorporate auditions in the big city into my independent study next semester. So ... I might need you to cover for me over winter break."

I'm a little confused, but of course I'll cover for her. I'm also sad that we'll be breaking our Christmas shopping tradition, but then I have a great idea.

"Hell," I offer, "Why don't I just go with you to New York? We'll go shopping together! Much better shopping up there!"

Hunter visibly winces at the suggestion.

"Hunter, what's going on with you?"

She puts on a brave smile. "It's complicated."

My breath comes out in a louder huff of indignance than I intended. "You could just be straight with your parents and tell them the truth. Then you wouldn't have to sneak off and make things complicated."

She cocks her head but keeps her eyes on the road. "Well, they're going to ask a lot of questions about where I might be staying and what I'm going to do for money."

"All valid questions. Do you have an answer for that?"

I watch her swallow nervously and take a sip from her water bottle.

"I just can't answer that right now, and I wish everyone would just give me some space to figure things out."

BUMMED AND CONFUSED, I can barely focus on swim practice, but I power through.

My social media embarrassment is overshadowed by the fact that my best friend is acting super weird. So weird, in fact, that she doesn't even show up to eat lunch with me under our favorite tree. We've been eating lunch together under this same tree since we started attending Greenbridge Academy in elementary school.

It's just as well; I'm not feeling hungry anyway.

WHILE COACH FORD spends most of practice going over the plan for our first meet this Sunday, I keep trying to get Hunter to make eye contact with me. For some reason she keeps darting her eyes over to Ridley, who is looking sullen and is quietly spouting off to Hadley about one injustice or another.

"And my dad's flying off to New York over Christmas, but I have to stay here in dumb old boring Greenbridge with my mom and her latest fiancé, plus the dorky soon-to-be step-sibling. Just the latest in her attempts to model the perfect, traditional family holiday for her Instagram followers."

Hadley says, "Yeah, but think of the guilt presents you'll be getting out of it from your dad! What do you think it'll be? Front row at Fashion Week?"

"Please. That was last year's guilt present. And anyway, I doubt he has any guilt at all. He's been acting really strange for the last month. He's suddenly got this whole thing about me needing a better work ethic, saying I'm not getting a new car for graduation, but he's instead gifting me his old Land Rover."

Hadley laughs. "And by *old* you mean, what? Five thousand miles?"

"I have busted my ass for how long and done everything my parents ever asked me to do, and I don't even get new car smell? I don't know what the hell is going on with him."

I glance at Hunter and she's positively green.

"Hunter, what is it? You look like you're going to ralph!" I whisper.

"It's too much to discuss at swim practice, I'll tell you that much," she says, anxiously tucking stray hairs back into her swim cap.

Coach Ford's voice booms over the whole scene. "If you girls are quite finished with your drama, we can get started."

I turn to glare at him. He is openly, brazenly staring at me. My eyes travel downward to his baggy board shorts. I can't see an outline at all, which is a damn atrocity.

Forcing myself to meet his gaze again, frustration heats my cheeks.

He purses his lips around the whistle, furrows his brow, and lets out one short blast.

"Here's how this Sunday's meet against Saint Mary's Prep is going to go..."

He continues, and I take it in while staring at him in challenge.

When he's finished, he asks if anybody has any questions.

For the first time in the history of swim practice, even going back to the age of twelve, I have a damn question.

"I do."

He raises one of his brows at me. "Shermer?"

"Yes, my question is... How dare you call us 'girls' and belittle our problems by calling it drama? We are fucking women!"

The howls of shocked laughter bounce off the water and the walls, but I pay no attention. I keep my eyes on him and he keeps his on me.

For a second he narrows them at me like he's considering what to do next. Considering what kind of punishment to dole out. He crosses his arms in front of him, his whistle in one hand. He presses it to his lips, just tapping it there as he thinks for a minute.

All my teammates are chattering because they still can't get over what I just said. Coach puts the whistle between his lips and gives a quick burst to silence everyone.

"All right, Shermer," he says, "it's about time you woke up. Stay mad, get your ass in the water and use that fire to show us what we can expect from you on Sunday."

I can hardly believe it. I just cussed him out—about as

heavily as I will ever cuss out anyone—and he's not going to punish me.

I hop on the platform and dive in at his whistle.

His loud, angry corrections through the bullhorn compel me to go faster, push harder, do better. The more he shouts, the more his stern voice echoes off the damp walls, the more I want to please him. And beg him to keep pushing me. To give me no mercy.

I want this man to ruin me. Wreck me. Take me in his office and break my cherry with his fingers. Oh my god, do I ever want that—the sooner the better.

When I've finished with my practice event and hoisted myself on to the pool deck, he marches up to me. My blood rushes and I gasp, but then realize he's coming over to show me the timer. He leans in close to show me my time on his watch. I pop my goggles onto my head and look closely, but all I sense is his cologne. This is as close as we've ever been to each other, physically, and it's everything I can do to keep my knees from buckling under the spell of his fresh, woodsy scent.

He speaks, leaning in closer to make sure I see my numbers. "Shaved off eight seconds, Shermer. I knew you had it in you."

I just stand there and breathe him in. Everything is falling apart around me. I'm sad, I'm angry, I'm confused. But I stand there for a few seconds and breathe him into my lungs.

Weston Ford. My torturer, my hero.

Before I can catch myself, my eyes flutter closed. It's just for a second. When I open them, everyone is staring at me—including him.

For a brief moment it feels like everything around us has

fallen away. The pool is gone, the people are gone. He and I are equals. And I feel calm. Everything is going to be OK.

"You OK, Shermer?"

I nod and turn away, harsh reality coming back into focus.

His voice is sharp again, booming, like he's preparing us for battle.

Somehow, he and I are going to happen.

It has to.

Or I might go mad.

10

WESTON

SO. She can stick up for herself.

Good girl.

I ask her to stay after practice; I have a valid excuse, because her first progress report is due for her independent study.

We meet in public because I haven't completely lost control of my senses. Her and I, alone in my office way back in the aquatics wing, is a recipe for shenanigans. So what am I thinking, asking her to meet with me now, instead of during school hours? The answer to that is simple: I just want to see her. Talk to her. Be near her.

She offers to meet me outside on the walking path of the school grounds.

I wait for Shermer by the main entrance with its massive limestone archway. When she arrives, she still looks salty.

Her face is still flushed and she looks put upon. This

might be the first time I've seen her dressed in anything except her school uniform or swim gear. Shermer's wearing a fitted v-neck sweater covered in polka dots and skinny jeans that show off the lines of her swimmer's body.

When she approaches me, I tell her, "You look full of piss and vinegar." It comes out dumb, not good-natured ribbing, as I intended.

"What?" She furrows her brow at me.

I wave it off. "Something my grandmother used to say about me. Forget it. Let's walk."

Shermer and I make our way along the stone walkways that encircle the high school building. The conversation goes as expected, as she fills me in on her progress on her project. Frankly, I don't care as much as I should, and most of it goes right over my head. But I do enjoy listening to her voice. She radiates confidence when she talks about things she cares about. Her eyes become fierce. The young woman who usually lacks confidence disappears and she shows me who she really is.

Before I realize it, we've walked away from the high school building and are clear on the other side of campus near the elementary building that served as a convent a long time ago. I pause to sit on a stone bench under the covered walkway near the bird-watching garden. A neglected, moss-covered statue of Saint Francis holding a bowl of bird seed watches over the place.

Shermer finishes catching me up, and I make the mistake of broaching another topic.

"We need to talk about the Facebook thing," I say before I lose my nerve.

She shifts uncomfortably on the stone bench. When I turn to look at her, I see she's mortified and angry. But I know the fierce, confident woman is still inside there, somewhere.

"This was a mistake," she says, her eyes blinking rapidly, like she's looking for something to stare at that's not me. "I should go."

Maybe she's right. "I'm sorry. I shouldn't have brought it up."

She sighs. "Just one problem. Hunter was my ride and she's gone. She couldn't even wait five minutes." I wish I knew what was going on with her. "Anyway ... God, I'm so stupid."

"Hey," I say. "None of that. I'd be lying if I said I wasn't flattered about the Facebook thing. There's nothing for you to be embarrassed about. But this thing between us is a non-starter."

She's blinking more rapidly and I realize she's fighting angry tears. *Non-starter? Good job using corporate speak when feelings are involved,* I think to myself.

"Shermer," I say.

Her breath is shallow. "Do you even know what it does to me when you bark my name in practice?"

The question hangs in the air. My better self reminds me that I'm in a position of authority. I can't entertain these kinds of questions. I can't — shouldn't — encourage her attraction to me. But there's another part of me that owes her some degree of kindness. I can't deny her the truth. "Yes. I know what it does to you. Do you want me to stop?"

Shermer shuts her eyes and breathes, "No! God, no! Don't you dare stop now."

I swallow thickly. This whole meeting was a bad idea.

"You know what could happen...what cruel rumors people could spread about you," I say, my voice wavering. "Let's just get you home."

Five minutes later, I'm alone with Shermer in my truck. This is an even bigger mistake than meeting with her after practice.

We spend the ride to her house in silence. She doesn't even question how I already know where she lives. Once I'm parked in her driveway, it takes all the strength inside me to keep my hands on the wheel.

"Thanks for the ride," she says in a near whisper.

"Sorry for embarrassing you. And sorry if it hurt that I blocked you. But I can't ..." I can't even finish the sentence without squeezing the shit out of my steering wheel and gritting my teeth so hard they might crack.

What the fuck am I doing? She can't be my car.

"I get it," she says. "I mean, why would you see me as a grown woman? To you I'm still that dorky preteen following you around at the city pool. I don't know why this is so hard for me to wrap my brain around—.."

"Stop it," I grit out. "I've told you before, stop running yourself down. It's not like that. You're not a kid. I don't see you as a kid ... not at all."

I shouldn't have said so much. Shermer swivels in her seat to face me.

Her gaze locks onto mine. The windows are down and the late fall breeze blows a lock of hair into her face. I know I shouldn't, but I raise my hand to touch it, to move it.

She leans in to me. God help me, she's leaning in and so am I. My heart is hammering in my chest. I can smell her citrusy, fresh scent. The same scent I dab on the end of my whistle so I can smell her all day long. Fuck me, I'm hard as stone right now and I can't do a damn thing about it.

Her wavy locks are the softest thing I think I've ever felt in my hand.

Shermer's eyes flutter closed. She has no idea what she's

doing to me right now. What does she think will happen next? If I so much as touch her skin, I won't be able to stop.

We're so close I can feel her breath on my cheek. She's visibly trembling.

Headlights sweep across the dashboard, startling us both. I fail to let go of her hair right away; instead I gently tuck it behind her ear as the automatic garage door rises in front of us.

The realization that someone has come home has Shermer snapping away from me, eyes wide and terrified. She's out of the truck and inside the house before I can say another word.

I back my truck out of the driveway just as Shermer's dad's Volvo slowly pulls in, his eyes straining to see who I am. I leave the window down, nodding and waving as I pull away. It's either that, or pretend I don't see him.

I make the choice that an innocent man would make. Because that's what I am, after all.

Totally, one hundred percent innocent.

11

ADDIE

THE FIRST MEET against Saint Mary's takes a turn I don't expect.

While we are prepping in the Saint Mary's locker room, Ridley makes an announcement.

"If I'm not going to swim the 100 freestyle, then I'm not going to swim," I hear Ridley say.

I'm shocked.

"What are you going to do?" I ask her as I rinse off the razor I'm using to shave my legs.

"What do you think I'm going to do?"

I stutter as I start shaving my arms. "You're...you're going to scratch? Hornets do not scratch, Ridley."

She steps toward me in the shower and snaps the strap of my competition swimsuit. "Your lady boner has blinded you to what is really going on here," she hisses.

I step backwards as if she slapped me. "What did you say?"

She chuckles. "It's so obvious. Oh, poor, sweet, innocent Adelaide. Top of the class. Every teacher's pet. Honey, please. It is all over your earnest, pouty-lipped face. Besides, I saw you leaving with him in his truck the other day."

I glance at Hunter, who's cutting her eyes at me.

I push past the fairly accurate accusation. "All right, fine, why don't you tell me why you're scratching?"

"Because I don't like Coach Ford. He pisses me off."

"I think he knows what he's doing. Nobody won us more state titles—"

"Almost five years ago. Things have changed since then. Competition is tougher. We need to play to our strengths, not try to make new inroads. I'm scratching to prove a point."

I back off and turn away.

I look at Hunter. She shrugs. "You too?"

"Nah, my mom would murder me," she says.

The decision by some of the girls to scratch does not go well for anyone. We lose to Saint Mary's, but based on the heats we did win, we could have easily won the meet if nobody had scratched.

The bus ride back to school is deathly quiet, and so is Coach Ford. It feels as though we are all waiting for him to let us have it, but he doesn't make a sound. When we arrive back in the lot at Greenbridge, Coach exits the bus, gets into his truck, and drives away.

Hadley breaks the silence first as she stands up to grab her gear. "Well, I didn't expect that reaction," she says.

Hunter and I exchange looks because we know what's really up. This gives me hope that she's still talking to me.

"Just you wait until tomorrow," I breathe as I watch Ridley exit the bus.

12

ADDIE

ANYONE WHO THOUGHT Coach Ford was going to let the scratched heats slide is sorely mistaken.

Monday morning, a flyer appears on the bulletin board from the athletic director: "Tryouts for girls' swim team alternates — tonight."

I know exactly what this means. People are getting suspended for what they did.

And I love it.

I think of nothing else all damn day except to wonder about how badly he's going to punish the team tonight. What's he going to say? And how loud? The tingling, quivering and dampness in my panties is almost too much to bear until school ends at 3:15.

13

WESTON

I SEE she wore her plaid uniform skirt today instead of khaki. And her nails are painted aqua blue.

The thought crosses my mind that I could quit my job right now, just for the chance to touch her. Just once.

14

ADDIE

BY THE TIME I don my swimsuit and get ready for practice, I am about out of my mind. I can hardly contain myself, wondering what is in store for practice today with half the team gone.

Coach Ford comes in hot to practice. His office door slams closed and he's already on the pool deck. He gives us a loud, sharp whistle, then barks, "In the pool. Butterfly. One hundred. Now."

One thing is clear—he is pissed.

At first I think he's warming us up but soon I realize he is flat out making us work. Hard. First butterflies, then the backstroke. And then breaststroke, followed by freestyle. And then just flip turns. "No! Shermer! You didn't even kick off the wall! Come on!" He's so mad he's not even using the bullhorn.

So angry. So damn hot.

When we finally finish, he doesn't even make us line up.

In our exhaustion he lets us stay in the pool, leaning against the sides, spread apart from each other in a sloppy line, catching our breath.

And then the thrashing really begins.

"Some of our teammates thought they could protest my coaching style by scratching their heats on Sunday. Some of our teammates thought they could get away with it. But they are wrong. Let this be a lesson to the rest of you…"

Oh man, he is just getting started. I… I really like this.

"Antics like yesterday? Got us spanked. Anybody pull that again on my watch, and you'll get cut from the team."

Oh…hell yes, I think, as the heat grows between my legs and my nipples tighten. I am going to rub one out to this later. Sure wish I could record this on my phone.

He goes on. "The following swim team members have been suspended for two meets: Ridley, Hadley, Daphne…" He goes on to name all six players who participated in the scratch yesterday. The uproar is immediate, but he blows his whistle. A vein in his forehead that I'd never noticed before swells and throbs as he points his finger at us.

"You brought it on yourself, ladies! You mess with my team? I'm the one who can mess up your entire future. Try me. Go ahead and try to send your lawyer daddies after me. You know what? I don't give a single shit who your families are. Do you know why? Because I got into this school on scholarship. I didn't belong here, and kids like you made sure I knew that since day one. But I earned my way onto the swim team and you better believe I worked my ass off. When the coach said jump, I said 'how high, sir?' Do you ladies have any idea how utterly privileged you are…"

Holy shit.

He goes on for at least ten more minutes, and I think the

water level of the pool shoots up a quarter inch as a result of how freaking wet this fiery speech is making me.

I inch my way away from the others and burrow into the corner of the pool.

Oh god. It's so wrong, but I can't handle it. I just have to...

My fingers push aside the elastic at the crotch of my swimsuit and brush my throbbing folds. My body reacts with a slight jerk. I delve in, massaging my swollen lips.

Coach Ford thunders on. "Our next meet is Sunday, and you may assume we are going to get pummeled because we're calling up alternates. Maybe we will..."

There's a pause in his tirade and I feel the skin on my neck prickle. I glance over at the pool deck and see him looking at me. All the eyes of my teammates are still on him, thank goodness. But he's got this look in his eyes that is something like unmitigated fury.

My thumb finds my clit and strums it. I stifle a gasp by biting my lip. My eyes flutter closed by their own free will. When I open them again, his arms are crossed and he's tapping his whistle against his top lip like he is thinking of what to say next.

He knows what I'm doing under the surface of the water. He has to know.

His brow furrows even deeper than normal. Then he bellows and looks away from me. "I say instead, now that we've cut away all the dead weight, let's move on and do our best. Because we are still the best. We still have the best program in the state, and we are going to relay so hard we're going to make Wakefield cry on Sunday!"

Some of my teammates are beginning to respond with whoops and claps. I'm just struggling to keep my facial expression under control as every circle of my hard little nub makes my nerve endings sing.

I'm close.

My lips part and I work to control my movements, praying nobody can tell what's going on.

The coach and I lock eyes again, and I do my level best to tell him with my gaze that I'm almost there. He has to know that each word out of his mouth only gets me hotter.

He finishes his pep talk with a menacing shout. "What are we?"

"Hornets!" My teammates' roar echoes through the room.

"What do we show?"

"No mercy!"

He makes them cry it louder and louder, over and over again, as my finger sinks into my opening. The pad of my thumb continues to rub, circle, and tease my clit until finally I explode with a cry at the same time my teammates are shouting "Hornets!" and "No mercy!" for the fifth and loudest time.

The climax barrels through me, mercilessly rattling my body. It starts at my pussy and travels up my back and into my chest. It feels like someone shot a glitter cannon in my brain.

When both the team and I finish, Coach Ford puts his whistle to his lips and blows. The rattle pushes out the final thrum of my orgasm. The walls of my sex respond to the slightest command from him, and it's all I can do to keep control.

He hastily leaves the pool deck, half jogging to his office, shouting over his shoulder, "Practice same time tomorrow. Be prepared to practice the relay with the alternates! Dismissed!"

15

ADDIE

COACH FORD IS ZIPPING up his duffel bag angrily when I pop into his office after practice. Hunter has agreed to wait for me so she and I can talk things through later.

"After tonight, I'm asking Frazier to assign you a different advisor."

"Why?" I'm thunderstruck.

"Because you're spending too much time around me and it's clouded your judgment."

That's not the reaction I expected. "But..."

He slams his locker door closed and I flinch.

"Go!" he shouts angrily.

The realization of my mistake hits me like a dive head first into the shallow end. My soul, my heart, my entire body hurts.

As I turn to leave, I mutter, "I'm such an idiot."

"Shermer, what did I say about that kind of talk?"

I turn to look at him and he's jangling his keys, anxious

to go, as if he hadn't just stomped my heart into a million pieces.

"Coach, I may be a decent swimmer and a great student. But when it comes to men, I clearly have no idea what I'm doing."

I swivel away as he says my name one more time, clearly regretting being so harsh with me.

"Shermer..."

I pause, not turning to look at him again. Just waiting to him to say something. Anything.

"Adelaide..."

My lip trembles, my back still to him.

"Adelaide, I wish things were different."

I don't respond. I physically cannot respond. I refuse to let him or anyone else see me on the verge of tears, so I bolt out of there as fast as I can.

I will never darken the doorway of his office again.

16

WESTON

THE CUTE REDHEAD on my doorstep is a sight for sore eyes. I let her in and wrap her in a hug.

"Hi, sis, glad you called today."

She lets go first and pushes past me. "What's for dinner? I'm starving."

"Nice to see you too, Barb," I laugh.

She putters around my kitchen as we chat, but then stops short when she sees the swim team photograph I have magnetized to the fridge. She pauses to examine it. "My brother the swim coach, haha! I've never seen you in khakis before. You look like somebody's dad."

"Thanks," I say, rolling my eyes, digging out the bottle opener from the kitchen drawer. "Somebody hired a professional studio photographer for our team photo at the beginning of the season. Guess they weren't satisfied with the yearbook club, for some reason."

"Oh... Is this her?" Barb points to Shermer immediately.

How in the world did my spooky sister figure out so fast the identity of the woman I've been texting her about for months?

I crack open two beers and hand her one. "Yeah."

She whistles, examining the photo. "She's absolutely stunning. I see the problem. Well, you wanted my advice, and I don't know what to tell you except what you already know. Based one what you've told me, this girl has it bad."

When I don't answer, she swivels around.

"Wes?"

I stare at the pot on the stove just beginning to boil for our pasta dinner.

"Almost as bad as I do."

Barb sighs and plops down on a barstool. "We're going to need something stronger than beer, brother."

17

ADDIE

THE BEST THING I can say about this humiliating afternoon is at least Hunter and I talked things out. I spilled everything to her about my meeting with Coach Ford. And she spilled everything to me about why she's been so cagey lately, which is a whole other story I'm still trying to wrap my brain around.

My plan is to get home, put one foot in front of the other, and hide out in my room until these swirling feelings pass. That plan is quashed as soon as I step inside the door. My mom and dad are waiting for me on the love seat, worried looks on their faces.

Open on my mother's lap is my diary.

"Oh. My. God."

"Honey," Dad starts.

"Why is Mom holding my diary!?"

"Let me finish. Your mother and I have been worried about you because you've been practicing so hard."

"First you want me to stick with swimming and now I'm practicing too much?"

He puts his hands up in surrender. "I know what this looks like..."

"It looks like you couldn't be bothered to sit down and talk to me and instead read my private journal."

Dad sucks both his lips into his mouth, as if he's trying to stifle himself from saying something he shouldn't.

"Dee, could you take it from here? I need to go put my fist through a wall if I have to say that asshole's name."

Mom puts her hand on dad's beefy arm. "Zeke. You're not going to put a fist through the wall over this." And then to me, she calmly says, "Try to look at it from our perspective. As parents, we know there's always risks when it comes to our child spending so much time with coaches outside of our supervision..."

Dad is now pressing the meat of his palms into his eye sockets as if to block out the mental image of whatever he's read in my diary. Oh god, what part did he read?

"What I'm trying to say is..." She holds up my diary. "Has Coach Ford made any advances on you?"

I squint. "Advances?"

"Has he touched you?"

"No!"

"As a coach, has he put his hand on you at all, even in a professional way?"

"No! God!"

"Has he given you any indication that he might be attracted to you? Made any comments to you about your body or the way you look? Found reasons to be alone with you?"

"Mother! No! He barely makes eye contact with me! I am totally, utterly fixated on him and he wants none of it.

And now I'd like to go put myself into a sugar coma and go to bed. May I do that?"

Dad is combing his fingers over his scalp, inadvertently giving himself lunatic hair. Mom puts her hand on his knee.

I stomp into the kitchen, grab a pint of ice cream out of the freezer, a spoon, and a tea towel to wrap the pint in so it doesn't melt too fast as I scarf down the whole thing.

"Maybe this was the wrong way to approach you with our concerns," she says as I tromp toward the stairs.

I stomp on the first landing. Turning, I smile at her ironically. "You think now, looking back, that maybe an ambush was the wrong move?"

Dad is grumbling and shaking his head, even after being assured Coach Ford has never tried anything and wants nothing to do with me, physically.

Mom sucks in a breath and holds up the diary. "So this...this writing is just fantasy?"

"Clearly! If it was more than that we'd be sneaking off together right now!" I gesture wildly with the ice cream.

Dad stands up. "That's it! I'm calling the AD! And then I'm calling Headmistress Moody, and then ..."

"Zeke, you will do no such thing," Mom insists. Dad paces back and forth. This power she has over him would be fascinating to watch if I weren't so angry.

I put my hands on my hips. "Wait a minute. Dad, weren't you Mom's teacher? Didn't you date Mom when she was seventeen and you were twenty-four?"

"She was eighteen and I was a student teacher!"

Mom nods her head. "And I wasn't a student. I had already graduated and was spending a gap year volunteering at the school before going to college. So I wasn't really a student. We were more like colleagues." She blushes deeply, which tells me part of her story is a lie.

I roll my eyes. "I'm going to my room."

I should just turn right around and head over to Hunter's. They could not stop me. But all I want to do is put on my pajama pants and hug my stuffed purple unicorn and cry and eat ice cream.

Worst. Day. Ever, I text to Hunter.

She texts back right away: *???*

M&D read my diary. Full of my pining re Weston. They are freaking the F out.

I'm texting her the entire saga when there's a knock on my door—two seconds before Mom pops in.

"Mom, I don't want to talk about this anymore."

"Neither do I. Put the ice cream down. Put your pants back on and come with me."

"What?"

"Just do it."

"Mom, it's a little late to drive me to reform school, OK?"

"Please. Just come with me."

I stare at her and I can see she's not mad. Well, how could this day possibly get worse?

"OK, just let me reply to Hunter."

To Hunter, I text: *Gotta go. Mom's taking me to Azkaban. Nice knowing you. Send chocolate.*

"WHERE ARE WE GOING?"

"To the doctor."

It's weird being in a car with my mom. Since Hunter and I got our licenses, I barely go anywhere with anyone but my best friend.

"I'm not pregnant."

"I know," Mom says, focusing on a left-hand turn by the hospital.

"Then why are we going to the doctor?"

"To do what I should have done as soon as you became interested in boys—putting you on the pill."

She pulls into the medical complex and begins searching for a parking spot.

"Mom, I haven't even had my period in three months, since I've been working out so hard."

"Oh, look, rock star parking, here we go. I know, honey. But that doesn't mean you can't get pregnant."

She parks the car and turns off the engine, and I'm staring at her like she's a witch.

"How do you know I haven't had my period?"

She sighs. "Because I'm the one who supplies this house in tampons, that's how."

"Good point."

She opens her door. "Listen, I don't know whether you're telling us the truth about Coach Ford. It doesn't actually matter. The point is, your body is obviously beyond ready to have sex, and it's time to take appropriate measures." She grabs her purse and puts on her lip balm while waiting for me to unbuckle.

"You're not mad?"

She turns to me. "This is not me giving you permission to pursue your coach, or anyone else. But...who knows what could happen. I want you protected because I love you."

"OK."

I go with her, but I save the "I love you, too" for when I stop being mad about my parents reading my diary.

18

ADDIE

I DON'T KNOW if it's the extra hormones in the pill, or the increased testosterone from training so hard, but I'm feeling more and more ornery lately.

I bury myself in swim practice and studies, determined to put Coach Ford out of my mind.

Despite missing six of our top swimmers after the awful meet against Saint Mary's, the alternates turn out to be pretty good. Hunter and I both place, essentially carrying the team to a win in the next two meets.

Ridley and her minions are fairly subdued and compliant at the next few practices.

All eyes are on the coach to turn this ship around, so I'm happy to leave him alone on a personal level for the rest of the season.

Fortunately, nobody seems to suspect anything untoward, and my parents evidently haven't told anyone about what they read in my diary. If they had approached the school with concerns, Ms. Frazier probably would not have denied Coach Ford's request to re-assign my independent study to another teacher advisor.

For my part, I turn in my weekly progress reports to his cubby in the main office, like a rule-abiding student. I don't speak to him at practice; I don't even make eye contact.

I follow orders, I swim my heart out, and that's it.

On days when he's particularly shouty and grumpy, and I find myself getting extra turned on, I take care of my problem in the privacy of my own bedroom late at night.

Dad is still pounding around the house, mad as a bear, but at least he stopped threatening to put his fist through Coach Ford's face.

Instead of writing in my diary, I've gotten into the habit of searching the internet for videos of Coach Ford swimming. There are loads of them since he swam in college and at world championships.

One of my favorites is of him swimming the 300 freestyle. The best part is when it's over and he launches himself out of the pool and punches the air. His tall, tan form is so jacked from hard work, and he looks so happy. I want to climb him that big, wet tree and let him soak my skin.

I have this fantasy that I'm his girlfriend in college, denying him sex before a meet, helping him shave his whole body.

"Babe, you're killing me," he says.

"You know everyone in the stands is watching you. Half of them want to fuck you, but I want you to remember who you belong to."

"As if I could forget."

The fantasy continues as I imagine his lips on me, while

in real life I'm snuggled under my blanket, pinching my nipple.

I'm falling asleep while trying to induce another wet dream when the text notification dings in my ear.

"Hunter, come on," I mutter.

But it's not Hunter.

This Addie?

I don't recognize the number. My heart drops a bit. It can't be Coach Ford because he would never call me that.

Who is this?

Roland Peek.

Captain of the men's varsity swim team. Holy shit!

I've never had a thing for Roland, but he's basically run the school from the age of fourteen. They say he could obliterate all of Weston Ford's speed records.

I text him back: *As in Ridley's bf?*

He replies, *Was her bf. Not anymore. What's up with u?*

I'm confused. I wonder what he wants.

Studying, I text back.

Same, same.

Need help with trig or something?

Nah.

Is there a swim thing I need to know about?

Nah, why do u ask that?

Bc you've barely said hi to me since 3rd grade & this is weird.

Nah, just checking in with u, girl. U know how it is.

I rarely know how anything is, I reply.

Ur funny. & cute. U know ur kind of the shit right now at school.

I roll over onto my stomach and tuck my plush unicorn under my chin as I read and text.

I'm the shit?

Don't be humble, it's too cute. Just wondered if u wanted to hang out sometime.

Is this really happening?

Are you asking me on a date?

U really gonna make me ask?

I roll my eyes. This fuckin' guy.

You texted me. The onus is on you to be clear with me.

He replies: *ROFL! U said onus. I didn't know u had a mouth on u.*

I cock my head and squint, trying to determine if that was a joke or he really doesn't know that word. I text back a bunch of eye-roll emojis as well as *Whatever.*

OK, OK, girl. Listen, Fisher's parents are out of town over New Year's. It's gonna be sick.

I twist my lips skeptically. *Sick, huh? Wouldn't Ridley have something to say about that?*

Ridley's cool with us moving on.

Hmm. A party might be fun. I roll onto my back again and rub my aching eyes. I have been working too hard.

Or does that crazy coach have you on such a short leash you're not allowed to have any fun?

The thought of Coach Ford literally pulling me around on a short leash is such a sudden turn on that my lady boner comes back with a vengeance.

I gotta get this turkey off the phone.

Something like that. Listen, I'll text you after Christmas and we'll decide then, Ok?

You're something else. See you then, Addie.

19

ADDIE

SINCE CHRISTMAS IS my favorite holiday, I try to focus on enjoying myself during the one week we have free from practice.

I miss Hunter, and I'm still worried about her, but I can't help but be happy for her as she sends me text updates from New York in the days leading up to Christmas. I'm skeptical about what's going on, but she seems good. I instead go shopping with my mom, and spend the days baking, decorating the tree and wrapping gifts.

To my pleasant surprise, Hunter returns home sooner than expected, telling me via text that she changed her mind and wanted to be with her parents on Christmas Day. Beyond that, she doesn't want to say much about New York, so I let it go.

"How was your Christmas?" she asks after arriving for an impromptu sleepover. I'm surprised she's not spending the night at her boyfriend's, and I wonder if something happened between them in New York. But I don't push; it's nice having her in my room again, rifling through my dresser drawer.

"Good," I say, nodding. "Serene. Uneventful."

She laughs as she pulls on a pair of my pajama pants and crawls under the covers with me. "Which means you are dying to get back in the pool."

I laugh. "Kind of."

"Bet you're looking forward to seeing Weston Ford, too," she adds.

I shrug. "I don't know. I kind of feel better not seeing him."

Hunter gapes at me.

"What?"

"Do you even realize how full of shit you sound right now?"

I disagree. "I'm not full of shit."

"Addie. I know you. You have it so bad for the man I can barely get you to look me in the eye right now."

I giggle. "You're crazy."

"If you can't be open with me, then there's no hope for you."

"You're one to talk. When are you going to tell your parents the name of your boyfriend?"

She replies with a big, dramatic yawn. "Oh...so sleepy."

"Whatever. Good night, nerd," I say, hitting her with my unicorn.

"G'night, butthead."

20

ADDIE

ROLAND PICKS me up in his Mercedes, along with two other guy friends in the back seat who aren't even a couple.

Honestly, I'm a little relieved that this really does seem to be a group thing, because I have zero interest in him.

When we arrive at Fisher's house, we have to park a block away because of all the cars.

At one time, I remember my mom telling me that when she and Dad were dating, he would drop her off at the entrance if he needed to park the car more than a few steps away. Clearly, Roland is not cut from the same cloth as my dad, which is just fine by me because I'm not in the least bit attracted to him, and this is not a date.

As we tromp down the street toward Fisher's house, Roland walks ahead of me with his bros, passing around a flask.

Strangely, I think Coach Ford is a lot like my dad. I bet he would be super protective and attentive on a date. My stomach flutters a bit at the thought of going on a date with my coach.

I wonder what he would wear.

I wonder what I would wear.

Would I put my hair up or down?

I bet he would bring me flowers.

I bet he would not only drop me off at the entrance to the party but also hold open my car door for me. And he'd definitely never walk five steps ahead of me.

We finally make it to the party. Roland disappears immediately, supposedly to get us drinks, but never comes back. Ridley and her gaggle of mean girls are there, eyeballing me but not speaking to me. I get the feeling Roland is using me to make Ridley jealous.

I wander around the party feeling like a nun in a sex toy shop. I just don't belong here, and soon I'm scoping the party for anyone I know well enough to give me a ride home.

Eventually I console myself with chips and salsa and find my way into Fisher's parents' library, where I settle into a wingback chair.

WESTON

RAY, the men's swim coach, pops into my office to tell me he heard about a big party tonight at one of his swimmers' houses.

"I know these kids think we don't hear the things they talk about in the locker room, but just wanted to give you a heads up. I think I heard something about some of your girls being invited. Knowing Roland and Fisher, there will probably be alcohol. Those twerps understand the consequences of their actions, but I feel bad for the girls getting dragged into it. You might want to talk to them."

I wrap up my work and log back into my computer, thanking Ray for the heads up.

I don't waste a single second in looking up where Fisher lives and staking out the place. No way in hell am I letting Shermer fuck up her life because of a dumbass party.

ADDIE

"COACH? What the hell are you doing here?"

I'm outside on the back porch, reading a book that I swiped from inside. Fisher's mom has quite the collection of bodice rippers. Coach Ford has appeared seemingly out of nowhere.

"Shermer. Who else from the women's team is here?"

Weird question but I'm intrigued. "Me, Ridley, Hadley, Daphne. I think that's it."

"Where's Hunter? I thought the two of you—"

"Hunter's with her boyfriend I think—that's all I can tell you."

"Oh." His steps are heavy on the slate stairs as he approaches. "Are you guys OK?"

I laugh. "Are you actually here to have a conversation about my teenage problems? But yeah, she and I are good. I wish she wasn't sneaking around so much, but she seems happy. Who knows—maybe she's got it figured out. Unlike me. I'll probably never understand my stupid feelings."

"There you go," he says, sitting down heavily on the wicker sofa next to me, "minimizing yourself. I don't like it."

I swivel toward him. "Care to tell me what you're doing here?"

"Taking you home."

I laugh. "Probably a good thing. Pretty sure Roland is drunk."

Coach Ford's hands clench into fists and I see a slight shake of his head. He's angry and disgusted. "Little fucker."

I laugh. "That's one way to talk about students at your school, sir."

"The school was full of shits like him when I was here."

"Yeah...and weren't you one of those shits? You were a god when you were a student at Greenbridge."

He shrugs.

"Seriously. I had a crush on you starting when I was thirteen. I used to sit under your lifeguard chair every summer and you never even knew I was there."

He laughs. "Oh, I knew you were there."

It's the first time I think I've ever heard him laugh. It's glorious. "You did?"

"Yeah. You've grown up a lot since then."

I blush, and I'm thankful it's dark. I look up at his face. He's sitting forward, his elbows on his knees, looking back at me. Even in the dark, his stoic face has me mesmerized.

He sits back so he's even with me, his eyes still on me. He blinks. I pivot my shoulders toward him. The night breeze gives me a chill.

Coach Ford removes his coat and puts it around me. When his fingers graze my shoulders, my whole body shivers. He pauses, his hands still holding the jacket sleeves. Am I mistaken or did he lean into me about an inch or so?

My stomach does a somersault. Is this happening?

The next second, the back door opens and Roland stumbles out, goes over to the bushes, and pukes.

The coach stands up.

"Go get the other girls, we are leaving."

I pop inside and tell Ridley, Hadley and Daphne a total lie that the cops are coming and that our coach is here to drive us home before they arrive.

When we start to pile into the truck, Roland hops in the back.

"This ride is full, son," Coach Ford growls.

Roland leers over at me from the truck bed, smiles, and pats his lap. "Got room right here!"

All of a sudden, Coach Ford hops out, comes around and grabs Roland, pulling him out of the truck bed.

"Take my advice. Stay here and sleep it off. Or, get in and I dump your drunk ass off on your parents' doorstep right before I text the AD that you've violated school rules about athletes and underage drinking. Your choice." Roland chooses to stay, thank god.

23

ADDIE

THE TEAM COMES BACK STRONGER than ever after
the holiday break.

The Hornets remain undefeated in the relay events for
the rest of the season. I finish first in the breaststroke,
Hunter medals in the butterfly, and Ridley snags first place
in the conference in the 50 freestyle.

We are headed to state by the time February rolls
around.

Neither Roland nor Coach Ford have been on my mind
in what feels like ages, other than in the context of
competition.

Yep. I've bottled up my feelings with a stopper made of
dynamite and put it on the back of a shelf made of match-
sticks on a hot day. But still, they're bottled up for now.

And then, the coach has us lined up for the morning's
pep talk outside the activity bus, and my silly fantasies start
to creep up.

"Ladies, visualize this as just another swim meet. But here's the thing..."

Here's the thing, Coach Ford, are you ever going to smile? I wonder if you'd smile when I step into your shower with you? I wonder what you'd like? Would you want me to go down on you first? Would you be patient with me, or bark instructions and pull my hair? Would you set the rhythm, force me to open up and let you go as deep as you want? Yeah, I've been watching sex videos so I know exactly what to do. I don't care if you never smile for me. But goddamn, I'm gonna make you moan.

I lock on to that feeling for the day's heats. And I crush them. I snap up medals in the breaststroke and butterfly. We place first in relays. Several of the girls medal and the Hornets win first place overall.

We are going back home state champions—a first for the school in over four years, and the first for the women's team ever. Hunter hugs me and she and I stand there on the pool deck and bawl our eyes out. This is it. This is what we've been working toward our whole lives since we learned to swim together at the city pool at five years old.

My best friend and I just won state.

I can hardly believe it.

On the way home on the bus, Coach Ford finally cracks a smile. He's sitting alone, looking at his phone.

I watch him, and I can't help but wonder who is putting that smile on his face.

If not the team, then who?

Something comes over me and I decide I no longer care about propriety. I slide into the seat next to him and hold out my hand.

He looks up, his smile fading. He looks...scared.

"What can I help you with, Shermer?"

Give me your phone."

"Excuse me?"

"Give it."

His brow furrows together but he actually hands it over.

His eyes are on me while I tap on his Notes app and write something only for him to see.

I've been on the pill for months now. And I'm a virgin. Whenever you're ready. You have until prom night, but that's your last chance.

I hand it back to him. He looks down and reads what I typed.

His lips part. His breath speeds the rise and fall in his beefy chest. "Shermer."

"What."

He glances around. "You can't talk to me like this."

I use my ace in the hole. "It's fine. I'm sure Roland is going to ask me anyway to make Ridley jealous. I guess I can go with him."

"No."

"What?"

The man has zero opinions about anything other than my swimming and my academics, denies me at every turn, but as soon as Roland's name comes up, he has opinions.

"How about a nice quiet kid from the Latin Club?"

I bat my lashes at him. "What's the problem with Roland? He's my age and we're friends now."

"You don't want to go with him."

"You can have an opinion about it when you decide to admit how you feel."

He goes back to looking at his phone idly, essentially telling me we're done here.

I go back to my seat to huddle with Hunter.

"What was that all about?" she asks.

"Nothing. It was nothing. Business as usual," I sigh.

WESTON

I'M SO DAMN proud of her. I knew she would bring home the title for us. Judging by her behavior on the bus ride home, she's finally seeing the same amazing, fierce, brave woman I see.

ADDIE

ALTHOUGH A PART of me would love nothing more than to drag out my independent study project until the end of the year as a convenient excuse to continue meeting with Coach Ford, I just don't have it in me. I've exhausted myself waiting around for him.

My heart still longs for him. My soul pines for him, and my skin yearns for his touch.

I still inadvertently moisten my lips whenever he strolls by in the halls, subbing for one class or another. My panties get wet when he's near and I smell his scent.

I still daydream, I still fantasize. But I've resigned myself to knowing that's all there is, and that's all there will ever be. If he wanted me, he would have allowed me to touch him. To get close to him. To open up to him.

All I've ever wanted was for him to see *me*, and now that I'm not swimming for him, he seems even less interested, if that were possible.

Until signing day.

"Honey, are you OK?"

Mom and I have ditched school this morning to shop for a dress for the signing ceremony. I've been offered an athletic scholarship to the nearby state university, and I've decided to take it. I could have accepted offers from more prestigious schools on both coasts, but I'm just not feeling as excited as I once was about going far away.

I give her my best smile. "I'm good. Just already feeling nostalgic for high school, I guess."

She looks at me like I've just suggested walking a tightrope across Niagara Falls.

"You? Feeling nostalgic about high school?"

I shrug and hold up a purple dress.

"It's a lot more...flouncy and flirty than what you usually wear, but I like it," she says.

I chuckle and toss the dress over my forearm so I can keep rummaging through the racks. "Are you saying I'm not feminine?"

"That's not even close to what I said. I like the dress. Would you like to try it on?"

I examine it again, then look back at the racks and racks of dresses, and decide I don't have the energy. I get so over-whelmed shopping for myself, I don't know how I am going to handle planning my own wedding someday. Maybe Hunter and my mom can do it. Honestly, I don't care a thing about dresses or makeup or flowers or what the cake looks like as long as there's a ton of good food—preferably hot dogs and burgers and lots of cheese. And carrot cake.

"This dress will work fine. If anything, it will be too big."

"That's the most sense you've made all morning. Come on, let's pay for the dress and then get some lunch."

"OK, but maybe just a salad. I'm not hungry."

Mom shoots me a look. "I've barely seen you eat since swim season ended. We're getting you a bucket of fried chicken."

We pay for the dress and examine the food court for the highest calorie food we can find and finally settle on noodle bowls followed by ice cream.

"You've been distant ever since you went on the pill and I feel responsible. Did I do the right thing?" Mom asks, half way through her bowl of mint chip.

I shrug. "Yeah, I think so. I mean, nothing is ever going to happen but it's probably a good idea nonetheless. But that's not why I've been distant."

"Are you having second thoughts about signing with state? Would you rather do it privately instead of having to sit next to Coach Ford? It's pretty stupid they have to film it for the news. I can call the whole thing off."

"I'm still interested in going to state. It's just that...do you think the TV camera will pick up on the feelings of a high school girl who is desperately in love with her swim coach and cannot do a thing about it?"

"Oh, sweetheart," Mom sighs.

"Are you going to tell me to get over it? Because I'm afraid it's hopeless."

Mom reaches over the table and grabs my hand. "Honey, I'm not going to tell you to get over it. I am going to tell you to do what you need to do to get through it. It sucks. It hurts. But if it's meant to be, you'll have your moment. I can't say when, and I can't say I endorse this, but if he feels the same way? Well, you're eighteen, you're about to graduate, and there's nothing I can say about it. But be prepared for disappointment. He's not going to want to lose his job over this, not after coaching a winning team."

"Thank you, Mom."

"I love you, honey."

"I love you too."

THE SIGNING CEREMONY takes place in front of four local reporters: one from the TV news, two from area newspapers and one from a local sports magazine. Our town is not a big city, but it's not small by any stretch.

Coach Ford and I are seated at a folding table that's been decorated with the school colors. Also there in attendance: a college recruiter, the state college swim coach, and a representative of the NCAA.

While the NCAA person is talking, I mutter to Coach Ford, "Slow news day, I guess."

I expect him to chuckle good-naturedly in response but instead I feel the heat of his gaze on me. I glance over and there's the signature look he gives me when I'm being self-deprecating. "Shermer, look out there," he says, gesturing to the crowd. "Do you realize you're the only scholar athlete in Greenbridge who's going to be on TV tonight? Memorize this moment."

Was that a wink? A smile? More like a grimace. I decide it's something close to a smile.

"Thank you," I whisper.

He dares to let his eyes travel downward. Just barely, but I notice it. His eyes land on my ruffled neckline. He sees me catch him staring, and he doesn't look away.

And then we are swept up in the signing ceremony and the moment is gone. My cheeks heat as I go through the motions, but all I can think is one thing: He likes my dress.

WESTON

PURPLE. My new favorite color.

I wonder what she'll be wearing to prom.

I can't imagine anything topping the outfit she wore today.

But my girl does the impossible day after day.

ADDIE

MY FINAL MEETING with Ms. Frazier and Coach Ford is in early April.

"I see you have your presentation in order for next week. Everything looks good. Coach Ford says you've not only been giving him monthly reports but also weekly, which is very good. I've looked everything over and I commend you, dear. It's great work."

"Thank you."

Ms. Frazier continues, "On top of that, miss state champion swimmer and scholar athlete extraordinaire, I have more news that probably won't come as a shock. You'll be graduating top of your class. I hope you've been thinking about what you would like to say in your valedictorian speech."

I blush and glance over at Coach Ford. His eyes flash and he appears to be biting the inside of his lip.

"Actually, no. I'm too sad to even think about all of this coming to an end," I say.

"That's quite sentimental of you," she remarks.

Ms. Frazier's secretary pokes his head in and gives her some kind of signal. For what, I don't know. "I'm sorry, I have to take this. Could you hold on for a moment?"

I nod my head.

While she pops into her office, Coach Ford and I are alone for an awkward moment.

"Shermer. Shermer, look at me."

I do, but hesitantly.

"I see what's going on in your head. You're embarrassed by all the praise. You've earned this. Enjoy it."

I look away. "I can't."

"Why not?"

"Because it hurts. Everything hurts. I bared my soul to you and it hurts my heart to look at you."

He shakes his head, and I think he's going to deny me one more time. "Shermer, it was an honor to coach you, and I'm so fucking proud to know you."

My eyes tear up. "Oh god. What are you doing to me? I..." Just then my phone dings. I check it, and it's a text from Roland. *Sup?*

I consider putting my phone away and answering him later but I would actually rather stop looking at Coach Ford.

I am grateful for the distraction.

I'm in Frazier's office.

Congrats, nerdictorian.

Idiot. How did you know?

Girl, ur the golden child, I keep telling u.

I'm overwhelmed.

As humble as u r beautiful.

Any girl in this school would feel honored, giddy to receive such a text from Roland. For me? Nothing.

I ain't buying what you're selling, Roland.

Ikr. Just putting my bid in for prom. As a group. Hunter should come with us. It's gonna be lit. No pressure.

"Prom." I say out loud.

"Prom?" Coach Ford repeats. "Who. Who is it? Fucking Roland?"

"None of your business."

"You're not going with Roland."

I can't believe we're even discussing this in the guidance office, of all places.

"If you don't want me, then I'm going to go with my friends. A bunch of the swimmers are going as a group. Surely you can't object to that."

He shakes his head and I think I hear his knuckles crack. "Someone needs to keep an eye on that kid."

"You lost your chance when you rejected me," I remind him.

When Ms. Frazier returns, Coach Ford makes a hasty exit, and that's the last thing he says to me for the rest of the school year.

Until prom night.

WESTON

TO: The Office of the Headmistress
    Subject: Prom
    From: WestonFord@greenbridgeacademy.edu

MESSAGE:

MS. MOODY,

I VOLUNTEER AS PROM CHAPERONE, no extra activity pay necessary.

OUR SENIOR PROM is at the opulent Ridley Hotel downtown.

Yeah, Mr. Rushmore named his flagship boutique hotel in his hometown after his semi-insufferable, spoiled rotten daughter.

But I gotta admit, even Ridley is being pleasant tonight, enjoying all the attention and real-time social media comments on her phone such as, "That place is almost as beautiful as you are!"

It's oddly freeing, spending prom night with my best friend. It's fun being dressed up, my hair, nails and makeup done, dancing, laughing.

Roland is here somewhere. He bought me a corsage that doesn't exactly match my dress or my personal style, but then again, he's left me alone to sneak off to the men's room with his bros to do god-knows what.

The Ridley Hotel is a massive, castle-like structure that looks old world on the outside but ultra-modern and chic on the inside, with outdoor Grecian-style gardens, pools, gazebos, a labyrinth, a koi pond, fountains, grape arbors, and many nooks and crannies for semi-private conversation.

It is all breathtaking, and I would expect nothing less with the name Rushmore attached to it.

But none of it compares to seeing Weston Ford in a tailored suit and tie. He's not my coach anymore, looking like that.

When he spots me from across the ballroom, his powerful legs eat up the distance between us. He stops short of touching me. We're maybe close enough for a handshake.

"What are you doing here?" I ask. "I thought you were leaving to train for the world championships this summer?"

"The AD was supposed to chaperone, but he had an out-of-town emergency and asked me to fill in."

I study his face. He looks slightly more drawn than normal. Like he hasn't been sleeping well. This care-worn face does nothing to diminish my feelings.

He's wearing a tailored medium gray suit with the hint of a pinstripe, a periwinkle pocket square and matching necktie.

"You look—"

"You look," he interrupts, "radiant."

I smile, turn red as a tomato, and drop my eyes to my gown. The fitted pastel chiffon flares out at the bottom, where it's dotted with a random pattern of wildflowers and accented with sequins. The dress has none of the cut-out patterns like most of the other girls on the team chose. I just can't do strapless and tight with cut-out designs. Mine is a bit more modest with a gathered criss-cross bodice and short sleeves that flutter when I walk. The plunging neckline is the only thing sexy about this dress.

"You look very handsome," I spit out.

His eyes drift down to my chest, and I feel my nipples react. "You look like a goddess."

It's then that I notice his pocket square and necktie are the same color as my dress.

I point to his necktie and back at my dress. "Hey, how did that happen?"

A smirk crawls across his face. "I have no idea."

My tomato-colored face is now the color of an eggplant.

"I hope you have a wonderful evening, Shermer."

"I've given up on wonderful, but I'm enjoying my time with Hunter, and that's all that matters."

30

WESTON

I WANT to ask her to dance, but if I dare touch her, I won't be able to stop.

The material of her dress almost floats around her dreamily; she could be living proof that magic is real.

"Save a dance for me," I say, but she's already walking away, back to her friends.

31

ADDIE

I HEAD BACK to my table where Roland and Ridley are lounging close together and speaking conspiratorially. She's got something in her handbag and I see her sneak it to Roland. It's a flask, of course.

I truly do not understand that relationship, and I don't think I want to.

The entire group takes a swig on the down low and I shock everyone by asking for a sip.

"There's my girl! Where've you been all my life?" Roland asks while everyone laughs.

"Shut up. We don't want the newbie drawing attention to what we're doing," Ridley remarks.

It's not the first sip of alcohol in my life. My dad occasionally lets me drink from his beer at backyard barbecues. But this stuff in this flask doesn't even taste good. However, it does sort of feel good after I force myself to swallow it.

I consider having another sip, but Hunter drags me out

to the dance floor. Our favorite hip hop song comes on and it feels good to be dancing with my best friend, just like when we were younger and used to act silly together in our pajamas and pretend hair brushes were microphones. I haven't felt silly in a long time, and it's needed.

After a while I start to feel sappy. "I'm going to miss you!"

Hunter hugs me. "I'm going to miss you!"

"Do you really have to leave right after graduation?"

"Yeah, the big guy is very impatient. Plus, I have another audition the day after, so he's flying me out there. You should come up and stay with me in New York over the summer."

"Yeah, but you're going to be working and going to school. I don't want to get in the way."

She grimaces and says, "Can you keep a secret?"

I look at her like she's lost her mind. "Can I keep a secret? Can I have a crush on my coach and tell nobody but you? Yes, yes I can."

"I'm not going to waitress. I'm not going to have a job at all."

I stop dancing. "And how do you plan on paying for acting classes?"

She spills all the beans in one single breath. "He's moving me into his penthouse and footing the bill for everything."

My jaw hits the floor. "You're kidding, right?"

She shakes her head.

I stop dancing and pull her to a dark corner. "Are you sure about this? Moving to New York for a guy is one thing, but moving in? That's starting to scare me a little."

She squares her shoulders. "Well, I'm not moving to New York for a guy, am I? I'm moving to New York to take acting and singing classes, remember? I'm just...relying on him to take care of things so I can do that."

"But you're pinning everything on him? What if he cheats on you? Dumps you? You know he has a bit of a reputation, right? Where will you go?"

She looks pissed. "First of all, thanks for the vote of confidence, and secondly, do you think I can't figure it out?"

I shake my head because I didn't mean it like that. I see Roland and Ridley slow dancing together out of the corner of my eye. Whatever. "I'm sure you will. I'm just worried that you're taking a huge leap."

She scoffs. "This from the girl who's scared of her own feelings. The woman who can barely look her crush in the eye. The girl who can't even notice that he's drop dead in love with you and you with him, and yet the two of you continue to waste time because of what everybody thinks!"

"Hunter, shh, someone will hear you." I look around to see if anyone's listening, but the closest people are bustling past us to go outside to the gardens, appearing to be quite drunk.

Hunter hisses. "I don't fucking care anymore. We are basically graduates already, so we can do what we want— don't you get that?"

I look around for Weston, but I don't see him anywhere. "He's made his feelings clear. He could lose his job."

"Maybe. Maybe not. And that right there is where we're different. I don't want to spend my life pining over something I didn't try," she says.

Her words sting. But I don't want her to see me cry.

Funny, she's the only person I usually do allow to see me cry.

"I need some air," I say.

"Addie," she calls after me, but I'm already outside.

She doesn't follow.

I find myself hiding in the garden behind the hedge that surrounds the swimming pool. Under a nearby rose arbor, a bench facing the marble fountains seems like the perfect place to cry. I'm not sure how much time passes, but eventually I sob my way through a whole packet of tissues. It's not saying much, since I could only fit so many tissues in my tiny clutch.

Out of nowhere, someone hands me a fresh tissue.

I reach up to take it and I see that it's Roland.

"Thank you," I say.

"Rough night?" he says. "I've been looking for you."

He smells like a distillery.

"I just needed some air." I don't invite him to sit, and yet he does.

A little too close.

"Roland, I—"

"Listen," he interrupts. "I know you have a thing for Weston Ford."

"What? No I don't."

"Come on. It's all over your face whenever you see him. Just let it go, OK?"

I glance around for the quickest exit. Maybe I can push him into the fountain if he gets too close. There's a little Cupid pissing water, and I'd love to see it pissing all over Roland right now.

"It's none of your business."

"I thought we were friends," he says, slurring his words.

"We're chummy acquaintances at this point. I wouldn't go so far as to say we're friends, Roland."

He laughs and scoots in closer to me. "That's good because I've had my eye on you all year and I'm planning on being more than friends."

I scoot away from him. A goldfish splashes in the koi pond nearby.

"Roland, I think you've got the wrong idea about me. I thought we decided we were just doing this as a group hang?"

"Yeah, but it's prom night..."

He leans in for a kiss, and I feel his warm whiskey breath on my cheek. "No."

He jerks back as if I've bitten him. "No? You're telling me no?"

"Correct. I don't feel things for you, Roland."

He doesn't back away. In fact, he gets closer. "Ridley told me you're a virgin." His voice is in my ear. "That's so fucking hot. See how hot you make me?" He grabs my hand and places it on his lap.

I am livid. I'm so angry I could nearly start crying all over again.

I jerk my hand away but his grip remains around my wrist.

"Let me go." More people are traipsing around the garden, and I can hear people making out not far away.

"You can't expect me to be a sad sack on prom night. You can't expect me to be celibate just because Ridley broke up with me."

I wrench my wrist free and try to stand up as I sneer, "Get the fuck away from me. I don't belong to you."

"You're my prom date, Addie." He pulls me back to him. I lose my footing and land in his lap. He regains his grip around my wrists and it hurts. I yelp.

"Not anymore."

It's what I was about to say but someone says it for me. Someone with a deep baritone voice with a crazed, murderous tone. Both Roland and I swivel our heads and see Coach Ford stalking toward us. He looks like his head is about to explode.

He grabs Roland by the front of his shirt and whips him backward into the hedge. If it had been a wall, Roland's head might have cracked open with the force. Instead, his body is pressed into the side of an oversized azalea shrub. The bright green leaves and bursts of hot pink flowers make a funny sort of crown around Roland's terrified face and I have to stifle a laugh.

Coach Ford is breathing rapidly, audibly, and I would not be surprised in the least if he is foaming at the mouth. Then he turns to Roland and speaks purposefully, just quiet enough to be terrifying. "You ever touch her again, I will cut off your puny little balls."

I look down at my wrists, which are red where Roland had gripped me. I think I would like to have a shot at removing his balls first.

"You're a fucking psychopath. My dad will have you fired for putting your hands on me." Roland's words are insolent but the spreading wet spot on the front of his designer slacks tells another story.

"Go ahead and try it, you little punk."

"You're history," Roland grunts before sprinting off around the side of the building.

We watch him go. My attention snaps back when I feel warmth on my cheek. The coach's hand is examining my face.

"Are you OK?"

I am shaking all over from the heightened emotions of the moment, from fear and confusion and surprise at his touch. He brushes my hair away from my eyes.

"Come on. I'm taking you to get checked out."

"For what?"

"For injuries. We need to document everything in case you press charges."

"Press charges? I'm fine! He barely touched me."

But he doesn't answer me. Instead he picks me up and carries me straight through the ballroom, out into the lobby, down the grand staircase, and out to the street where his truck is already waiting.

I'm reeling from being carried by my swim coach across the dance floor to the utter astonishment of all my classmates. And there's no sign of Hunter anywhere.

He puts me in the passenger seat gingerly and snaps the door closed. In another few seconds we are speeding down the highway to the hospital.

I open my purse and pull out my phone. I calmly tell my shocked parents that there was a fight at prom, that I'm perfectly fine, and that they should meet us at the emergency room, where I will explain everything.

This whole situation is so ridiculous, so over the top, it reminds me of the romance books I read late at night when I can't sleep. He actually carried me like a distressed damsel out of a ballroom in front of everyone I know. It occurs to me that maybe I've manifested this man from those books. Maybe Weston Ford isn't even real. Maybe I made him up and this is just a dream, a long, angsty, slow burn kind of dream that never pays off in the end.

I can't help it, I get the giggles. I cover my mouth and snort. And then the guffaws come loud and fast, and I'm doubled over in my seat.

"Shermer," he rumbles. "Are you laughing or crying?"

A tear trickles down my cheek and I say, "I don't even know anymore. This is not how I envisioned my prom night ending!"

32

ADDIE

IT'S ALL OVER.

I'm finished.

My eyes scan the audience in the vast auditorium. He's not here to see me graduate.

At the hospital after prom, he handed me off to my parents, and I didn't see him the rest of the night. I didn't see him at school during the days following prom. I moved through the last weeks of my high school career in a fog, highlighted by comments and whispers here and there from people who had seen me in his arms on prom night.

My valedictorian speech is brief, funny, inspiring— everything everyone expects of me.

But my heart is on the floor.

We won't get our happily ever after.

I was so sure there was something real.

Is it his fault? Had he been giving me hope all this time, or was I seeing signs that were not there?

I take my diploma and shake hands with the head-mistress. I'm the only student she hugs, and it's such a tight squeeze, it makes me regret not getting to know her better.

Why did I waste my mental energy this whole school year? These people believed in me and I didn't treasure them. I never took the time to create a mental picture of my last year of high school.

Yes, I aced every class. Sure, we won the state title.

But I did it for the wrong reasons.

From now on, I resolve to succeed for myself, not to get the attention of a man who doesn't even care about me.

I brush past the black curtains at stage left to make my way through the backstage area toward the side door of the building. No way I'm going back to my seat.

Before I reach the door, something clamps down around my wrist. I gasp in fright. It's a hand, and for a split second I think it might be Roland. The hand around my wrist tugs me through the back curtains and toward the shadowy edges of the stage.

My eyes finally adjust to the backstage darkness, and I see what's happening. That hand on my wrist is attached to the world's most beautiful and exasperating and wonderful human.

I feel as though I'm being lifted outside of my body.

Weston Ford has me.

Without warning, he releases my wrist and takes my face in his hands. He claims my mouth in a ravishing, angry kiss.

His hand lets go of my face and his arms wrap around me so tight I am exquisitely out of breath.

My feet rise off the floor.

Every resolution I just made flies out the window.

His lips, his sweet breath, his fresh, woodsy scent, is everywhere—on me, inside my lungs.

I know that half a dozen of my classmates are filing past us just on the other side of the curtain. Surely someone will see us.

But they aren't my classmates anymore. They are former classmates.

And I'm no longer a student.

"Adelaide," he murmers into my mouth.

His low, gravelly voice makes my body shudder in response.

I savor this moment. I take a mental picture of it. I memorize what his lips feel like against my lips, what his strong fingers feel like as they dig into my hips. His hard length presses against me so tight I feel it in my bones.

"Weston," I breathe into his kiss. I have to, since he's not letting me break away to speak.

We're moving.

I can't see where he's taking me, but I no longer care who I am, let alone where we are going.

33

WESTON

AFTER CARRYING her into the abandoned prop room deep in the bowels of the auditorium basement, I grip the front of her white graduation gown with one fist and unbuckle my jeans with the other. I should slow down, kiss her tenderly to prepare her for me, but it's too much. I can't hold back. I've got her pinned against the wall in the darkened room.

"Sweetheart, this is not how I wanted your first time to be, but—"

She quiets me with a quick kiss before saying, "You don't have to be sweet to me. Do what you need to do. Wreck me."

A noise escapes me that's part joy and part mad beast.

I hike up her robe and her dress.

Adelaide puts her arms around my neck, one hand still gripping her diploma while I hoist her legs to wrap around me.

I back her up against the chipping ivory paint on the cinder block wall. This isn't good enough for my sweet girl but my blue balls are beyond caring.

To hell with it. Not even the Four Seasons is good enough for my princess.

When I've got her firm ass cheeks in my hands, she grinds against me, and I respond with an angry roar and rip away her flimsy panties. My hand finds her warm, wet pussy and the touch makes her moan into my mouth.

"Hold on tight, baby."

She grips me with her thighs like she's climbing a tree. I use my free hand to spring my cock from my boxer briefs, and it can't find her core fast enough.

"I need you now," I rasp into her mouth.

She whimpers. "Yes please, god. Oh god, yes please."

I don't wait another second. My cock swells as the tip finds her entrance, and I dive in.

She urges me on with a squeeze of her thighs, a thrust of her hips.

"I'm gonna break you and it's gonna hurt."

"Fuck you. Nothing can hurt me more than spending months heartbroken over you."

Fuck. I cram into her all the way and feel her barrier break. She cries out, but squeezes me, urging me to keep pushing. I kiss her mouth. She's so unbelievably tight it almost hurts.

I slide out all the way and push back into her with so much force that her mortar board is flat against the wall.

"Yes! Weston!"

Her words ramp me up and soon I'm flat out fucking her at a frenzied pace.

Her pussy is soaked, and the harder I fuck her, the

louder she moans. Her pussy sucks me in and it feels so damn good to claim her. Finally.

"Fucking torture. Fucking prom dress. Fucking flirty purple dress. Fucking masturbating in the pool right goddamn in front of me. Why the fuck did you think I was so damn mad all year..."

Her body writhes against me. She kisses me so hard her tongue nearly goes down my throat.

She's breathless when she speaks. "I love it when you're mad. Show me how mad you are at me."

Her words send me over the edge and I fucking nail her. Her hips roll into me like a champ. Is there anything this woman cannot do right when she puts her mind to it?

"Hold on tight, sweetheart, it's gonna get rough."

"Oh god, please."

The pace of my thrusts ramps up until her words all bleed together. Her moans are drowned out by the animalistic grunts spilling out of me. I have no idea where these sounds are coming from. She has unleashed the beast and the beast is going berserk on her sweet virgin pussy.

It's so wet, so tight, so sweet, her mouth so soft and tender, there's no other one for me.

My balls tighten. I'm going over the cliff.

She squeezes me harder with her athletic thighs. "Don't pull out, Weston."

"Woman, you ain't a parking lot. No way I'm pulling out."

And I'm jetting inside her. Filling her with my cum.

My cock has wanted this all year; it's coming coming with a pulsing release. Her pussy matches me with every pulse, clamping down to suck in every last drop of my juice.

"I love you, Adelaide. I love you so much. You're mine, you've always been mine."

She hugs my neck and breathes into my shoulder and it warms me through the material of my shirt. "I've felt it from the beginning. I have loved you since I was fourteen years old, Weston Ford, and I'll never stop."

34

Adelaide

HE RUMBLES, spent against my chest, his massive cock still lodged inside me. "I'm taking you home."

"What? After that? I don't want to—"

"My home."

"Oh. Well, I don't think I can walk."

"I'm offended you don't automatically assume that I won't do this." Weston scoops me into his arms after putting away his cock and zipping up, somehow while still holding me astride his hips.

My pussy feels the empty space where he was inside me and it's not happy.

I let out a whoop of surprise when I find my legs in the air, his arms cradling me under my legs and my lower back.

"I've got you, sweetheart."

Just like on prom night when he thought I was injured, he carries me out of the building and across the parking lot to his truck.

I want to say I can't believe it, that I'm finally Weston's girl.

But I can.

I totally can.

At the beginning of the swim season, Weston told us swimmers to visualize what we wanted, so I did. My entire senior year has been like this in my head. I pictured him taking me up against the wall. I pictured him scooping me up in his arms and carrying me to his truck.

My parents are standing outside, glancing around to find me in the crowd of celebrating families and graduates. Everyone is taking selfies, but then a few people turn to look our way when they see us exit out the backstage door.

My mom and dad turn and spot me. Dad looks like he's going to come after us but he halts with one touch to the arm from my mom.

"I'll be back tonight for the graduation party!" I call to them.

WESTON SMOOTHS a hand up the inside of my calf, up the inside of my thigh.

My dress, cap and gown are tossed aside.

He's pulled down the lace of my bra to suckle my breasts, and I help him by reaching back to unfasten the hooks. It pops off me; Weston's hands cup my breasts and he stares at them in awe.

He's going so slow right now, I might faint.

Soon enough, his hands press my thighs apart.

It's only been minutes since he was devastating my pussy against the wall of the auditorium, but now my lady bits are quivering for it. For him.

His fingers swipe teasingly over my pussy lips, combing through the small patch of short curls.

I gasp at the sensation of his fingers there. Every nerve ending in my body reacts, causing goose flesh to appear.

"You're so beautiful, Adelaide," he whispers, his fingers tickling my curls. He runs the back of his knuckles over my slit and he curses. "Shit, do you realize how wet you are right now?"

I let out a moan.

I feel his thumbs on either side of my slit. He spreads me open and slowly, tortuously, runs his tongue from my entrance all the way up to the small, desperately hard nub.

"I'm so looking forward to getting you off, baby. I've been looking forward to tasting you on my tongue, swallowing all your juice, and then filling you up with my cum."

I feel my body blush at his words. "I doubt you have any left after the way you fucked me in the middle of graduation," I say, reveling in the sensations of his mouth, lips and tongue tasting, devouring, suctioning and nipping away at every inch of my pussy. "Oh my god, Weston. Am I in heaven?"

35

WESTON

SHE TASTES the way she smells—juicy and sweet. The more I drink her in, the more she drips for me.

I murmur against her skin between mouthfuls. "Of course I have more where that came from. Do you know how many times a day I jerked off to thoughts of you?"

Her voice is ragged. "Oh...wow..." Her hips arch up toward me, like she can't get enough of my mouth against her pussy. Like the friction is just not enough. I understand that need.

I pull away briefly. "Ask me."

"Uhm. What? I don't remember the question."

I can't help but feel a little proud of myself that I've made her head so cloudy. "Ask me how many times a day I jerked it to you."

"How many times?"

"Three times every damn day."

"All year?"

I don't answer her right away but instead suction my lips around her clit. The small nub feels good and tastes like heaven. I let it pop out, causing her to squirm and cry underneath me.

"All year. From the moment I saw you. I've been obsessed with you. Now tell me, princess, how many times did you rub one out in my pool?"

She gasps. "Never!"

I sit up on my haunches and look her dead in the face. "That's a lie and we both know it. Were there more times besides that time in practice in front of everyone?"

"Weston! Please!"

"I'm not going to finish you off until you admit you were touching yourself in the pool while I was yelling at everyone."

"Fine! Fine, I admit it!"

I smile wickedly while I proceed with the business at hand, my lips returning their attention to her swollen clit. I make her moan and writhe and drip with every bit of pressure. Every nibble elicits a juicy noise from my wanton woman's throat.

"God, fucking you every night for the rest of my life is gonna be so amazing."

Her thighs tremble. She's getting close. "You knew I had to touch myself. I couldn't take it anymore. Oh! Oh my god!"

She shouts and gasps as I slide one finger into her channel while I continue to gently suckle her clit. I curl my finger and hit her spot on her inner wall, while ravaging her folds and her clit with my tongue and lips, sucking, gently biting. She sucks in her breath, bucks her hips hard against my face, and screams out her orgasm. Her pulsing walls clamp down around my finger, as her juices squirt and her back arches. My free hand slaps the meaty part of her tight bottom.

She yips in pleasure, and her hands reach for my face. "I want to see you. I want you to see what you've done to me."

How can I say no? I scoot up to come face to face with my Adelaide. Her face is flushed, and her eyes are glazed over. I gently touch my lips to hers, letting her taste herself. She accepts the kiss and then looks in my eyes with so much pure, unfettered love.

"Sweetheart. My sweet girl."

She cups my face and deepens the kiss, wrapping her legs around me, nestling me close to her.

She pulls back with a smile. "It feels like you're ready to go again."

"I'll always be ready to go—any time, any day."

I lift her hips toward me and slide my cock inside her. She's still so tight and wet, it's just like the first time. She fits me perfectly.

Unlike last time when I fucked her against the wall, this time I take my time, thrusting with long deep strokes, while running my palms over her ass, her legs, her torso, up to her round, full breasts. I suck her taut nipple into my mouth and I'm pleased to find it's sensitive enough that her thighs and her pussy respond when I do this. I lavish the other nipple with the same attention as I memorize her graceful curves, the unbelievably soft skin against my hands. I nuzzle my lips, tongue and face against her breasts.

Her small moans, gasps, and throaty squeaks grip my heart.

"You're mine—do you understand? All mine. Nobody else is allowed to touch you, not ever. You belong to me and only me."

"It's all I've ever wanted, Weston. I was built to be yours."

I give one sudden hard thrust and her brows knit together while a smile creeps over her lips, now swollen from kissing.

"Just one more thing I need from you," I growl.

"Mhmm," she responds, her eyes closed, lost in pleasure.

"I want you off the pill."

Her eyes fly open but she doesn't stop meeting my thrusts, nor does she look offended.

"I love you and I want to put babies in you immediately. I want a lifetime of babies and grandbabies and great-grandbabies with you."

She bites her lip and tears well in her eyes. "I want that too. I want all of that. Give me all of your little swimmers, coach, I'm ready when you are."

With that, I rub the pad of my thumb in circles around her clit until she shatters around me. I come as well, rocketing even more of my seed into her than last time. She cries out, while I grit my teeth and roar with every pulsing release. There's so much of it, I don't care what kind of birth control she's on.

My swimmers are just like me: fucking champions.

36

ADDIE

AFTER A MIND-BLOWING afternoon spent in Weston's bed, I definitely cannot walk.

My Weston takes me to the shower and tenderly cleans me up under a hot spray, still managing to lavish my body with attention even though I can barely take any more. He helps me get dressed and is ready to carry me to his truck but I insist on walking.

"I am going to have to get used to having the strength taken out of me. I can't go around helpless for the rest of my life."

"Yes, you can," he says. "I'll carry you after I make you go limp for the rest of my life, sweet girl."

I sigh happily all the way back to my parents' house—just this morning it was my house—while holding his hand. We take turns kissing each other's hands all the way there like a couple of nerds. And it's so damn sweet I don't have time to notice my nerves until we pull up in front of the house, my graduation party in full swing.

Weston anticipates my anxiety and squeezes my hand.

"Everything is going to be OK. Even if your dad beats the shit out of me, it's going to be OK. Say it."

I take a deep breath and repeat what he says, secretly praying Dad doesn't actually take a swing at Weston.

He hops out and dashes over to help me out of the passenger side.

If I was nervous a second ago, it dissipates when his hands grip my waist to help me hop down. It's a small gesture but it feels so natural and so correct. I have nothing to worry about because we are the perfect fit.

As we approach the house, all eyes are on us and my stomach does a somersault. It does a backflip when my dad emerges from the back door, a Coors Light in his hand.

He's pissed.

Mom's eyes are darting between me and Weston and Dad, wondering what's going to happen next.

"Sir," Weston starts.

Someone has turned down the music by the pool because, of course, everyone wants to hear this.

"No, I talk first," Dad says.

I swallow hard and look at Mom. She shrugs like she hasn't been able to suss out Dad's feelings all day.

"My baby girl has had a crush on you since the beginning of the school year. Maybe longer. If I ever hear of you breaking her heart or standing in the way of what she wants to do with her life, I will hunt you down and I will end you. End. You. Do you understand?"

I look at Weston, and he is resolute. His brows knit together.

"Sir, I'm marrying Adelaide. I've been looking for her

my whole life, without even realizing who or what I was looking for. And I would argue that she's not a baby girl. She's a grown woman with choices. She has her whole life ahead of her—her choices are limitless—and any person who would stand in the way of that is a fool. And by that I mean, anyone who would stand in the way of her career, her education"—Weston pauses—"or her relationship."

The two men I love most stare each other down for a few moments, but neither of them breaks. Finally, Weston puts his hand out. Dad looks at it, looks at Weston, and takes it.

I need not worry about everyone gaping at us for the rest of the night. Moments later, Hunter shows up with her new beau, and their story is the real head turner of the party. Thank god for my best friend, who knows how to create a diversion whether she means to or not.

She introduces me to him, even though I know who he is. I try not to giggle, but I'm so surprised and overwhelmed.

"Come on, let's have some cake," I say to them.

After giving a short speech to thank everyone for coming, I cut up the cake and serve it. Half carrot cake with cream cheese frosting—my favorite—and half lemon with lemon curd and buttercream.

I have a huge piece of both as Weston murmurs in my ear, "Eat up, buttercup. You'll be eating for two soon."

I laugh and nearly choke on the icing. "Too soon. It's going to take a couple of months at least for my hormones to get straightened out."

He laughs and inhales my hair, bending down to kiss my neck.

"We'll see about that."

EPILOGUE

WESTON

WELL, I wasn't precisely correct about the timing, because it did take a couple of months to get pregnant. But by the time I move her into my house and take her to her first class at the university, she's already battling morning sickness.

Even having thrown up her breakfast, my angel—my wife—is still as stunning as ever. So stunning that I can see other dudes on campus checking her out as we walk to her classes.

One guy walks over and hands her a flier for a party at his fraternity.

"Nice! Thanks!" she says.

Like hell. I snatch it from her and shove it in the nearest recycling bin.

"What was that all about?"

I hold the door open for her. "He was hitting on you."

"No, he wasn't, he was inviting me to a party. He was being nice!"

"Trust me, I know these guys. And besides, you can't drink in your condition."

She rolls her eyes at me but I can't help it. She's mine and I trust her completely, but it's other dudes—especially fraternity dudes—who I don't trust.

Later that night when we're lying in bed, she reminisces about our wedding. The guest list was small, but Hunter served as our maid of honor, and I'm so happy the two of them made amends after prom.

Our wedding was held at Hunter's boyfriend's estate on the lake and turned out more extravagant than either of us expected. The man had insisted on letting his household staff plan the wedding.

We got married under a huge white tent, with white flowers and curly willow everywhere, and all the chairs were covered in huge silk bows. The lake had been filled with floating lanterns. The entire swim team was there, even if Ridley was looking a bit salty and wore a white dress. She tried, but she paled in comparison to my bride, who looked like a goddess. And it wasn't just her dress. She glowed with love for me.

"Hmm. I still can't believe he found someone to make mini bacon-wrapped corn dogs. I would kill for one right now," she murmurs while she strokes my hair.

I shake my head. "No corn dogs for you. No cured meats at all—remember what the doctor said?"

She slaps my chest and giggles. "Nothing gets by you, does it?"

"See? You do need me to take care of you at college. You'd be eating soft cheese and deli meat every day if it weren't for me."

I hear her belly growling as she says, "Oh man, I bet the

guys at Beta Psi have soft cheese and deli meat. Maybe I'll go over there. And beer, and sushi..."

I roll on top of her to plant a kiss on her mouth.

"I got something for you."

I pop into the kitchen and take the plate I've been keeping warm in the oven ever since she came home from classes.

She pouts. "But you said I can't have hot dogs."

"It's a faux hot dog, made with vegetable protein, wrapped in soy bacon."

She smiles bravely and sits up, taking the plate.

"You've been craving hot dogs since the second you got pregnant, so I thought this might be the next best thing."

She picks it up, sniffs it, then sets the plate down on the side table.

The next thing I know, she's shoving me on my back, and what can I say? I have to let her. She straddles my legs and runs one hand up my thigh to warm the bulge in my jeans.

"You misunderstand me. Did you know that it was exactly one year ago today that we had our first swim practice together?"

I'm having a hard time concentrating with her hand slowly rubbing over the hard length of my dick.

"Yeah, I remember that day."

"It wasn't long after that I was staring at your giant boner on display in those cute-ass tight swim trunks."

She gives my cock a hard squeeze and I suck my breath in through my teeth.

"I remember, Shermer."

"Good. Then you know there's only one sausage I crave."

"Dirty girl."

"You don't know the half of it."

"Really? What else you got?" I ask, playfully suspicious.

She hops off me and trots over to the nightstand and pulls out three objects: my Greenbridge trunks, my clipboard and my whistle.

I laugh. "What am I supposed to do with all of that?"

"Boss me around, Coach. Just the way I like it."

THE END

THANK you for reading Swim Coach. If you enjoyed this short story, please visit my website at authorabbyknox.com for links to all my books. Keep reading to find out where to track me down on social media and email, or sign up for my mailing list to be the first to know about upcoming projects.

ABOUT THE AUTHOR

Abby Knox writes feel-good, high-heat romance that she herself would want to read. Readers have described her stories as quirky, sexy, adorable, and hilarious. All of that adds up to Abby's overall goal in life: to be kind and to have fun!

Abby's favorite tropes include: Forced proximity, opposites attract, grumpy/sunshine, age gap, boss/employee, fated mates/insta-love, and more. Abby is heavily influenced by Buffy the Vampire Slayer, Gilmore Girls, and LOST. But don't worry, she won't ever make you suffer like Luke & Lorelai.

If any or all of that connects with you, then you came to the right place.

Join Abby's newsletter
and say hello at authorabbyknox@gmail.com

Milton Keynes UK
Ingram Content Group UK Ltd.
UKHW020730030823
426269UK00014B/507